20-8-5
6-1-20-8-5-18
9-19
4-5-1-4

D1059049

"I thought you at least had SOME sense of honor—in your sick, twisted way! HOW COULD YOU DO THIS?"

CAHILLS vs. VESPERS

TRUST NO ONE

THE 39 CLUES

LINDA SUE PARK

SCHOLASTIC INC.

To Steve Mooser and Lin Oliver,
with affection and admiration.
— L.S.P.

The author gratefully acknowledges
Dr. Kathryn James at the Beinecke Rare Book and
Manuscript Library at Yale University for her
help with the researching of this book.

Library of Congress Control Number: 2012939109
ISBN 978-0-545-32415-1
10 9 8 7 6 5 4 3 2 1   12 13 14 15 16/0

Book design by SJI Associates, Inc.
Book illustrations by Charice Silverman for Scholastic.
Voynich page p. 16: General Collection Beinecke Rare Book and Manuscript Library,
Yale University; blow dart p. 98: © Marilyn Angel Wynn/Getty Images;
Metal texture for dog tag p. 173: CB Textures.

Library edition, December 2012

Printed in China 62

Scholastic US: 557 Broadway • New York, NY 10012
Scholastic Canada: 604 King Street West • Toronto, ON M5V 1E1
Scholastic New Zealand Limited: Private Bag 94407 • Greenmount, Manukau 2141
Scholastic UK Ltd.: Euston House • 24 Eversholt Street • London NW1 1DB

CHAPTER 1

The plane made its final approach into New York City. It was morning on this side of the ocean. Who knew what time it was in Timbuktu now?

Along with his sister, Amy, and two friends, Dan Cahill was a passenger on a private jet. The jet was owned by their distant cousin, hip-hop superstar Jonah Wizard. As Dan gazed out the window, he downed the last of the fresh strawberry and pineapple smoothie made to order by the cabin attendant.

It was a pretty amazing way to travel.

Dan leaned sideways a little to get a clearer glimpse of the skyline. He loved the view of all the iconic structures: the Empire State Building, the Chrysler Building, the Brooklyn Bridge.

And most of all, the Statue of Liberty, standing proud in the harbor. Dan would never have admitted it out loud, but whenever he flew into New York, he always felt like she was welcoming him personally, as she had so many travelers before him.

The cabin attendant, a calm and efficient man

named Victor, came by to take Dan's empty glass. He leaned over Dan's shoulder and pointed out the window toward the southern end of Manhattan.

"That's where the towers used to be," Victor said. "The World Trade Center buildings. You probably were just a baby when they went down."

It was true. Dan had never seen them in real life, only on video. It was easy to recall the footage from that day in September of 2001: the hijacked plane crashing into the first tower, then the second, gouging huge, jagged holes into the buildings. Floods of black smoke and fierce orange flames everywhere.

Even more horrific than the crashes themselves were the unbelievable moments that followed, when both of the massive superstructures collapsed and crumbled into dust, as if they were no sturdier than sand castles. The first time Dan saw the footage, he thought it looked like something out of a Hollywood action movie.

But it had been all too real. Nearly three thousand people had died.

"That part of Manhattan always looks so empty to me now," Victor said.

The southern end of Manhattan was hardly empty. There were hundreds of buildings massed together, short, tall, taller. It reminded Dan of a crowd jammed into one of Jonah's concerts: The tallest buildings were like the people who sit on their friends' shoulders so they can see better.

It was hard to imagine how or where two massive towers could have squeezed into that jumble.

"So sad," Victor said, "the things people will do to each other."

Dan sat back against the seat cushion and let out a sharp breath. Victor's words had hit him like a body blow.

The Vespers.

They had already done terrible things to people Dan cared about. If they got everything they were after . . . Dan couldn't imagine what they might do next.

He had to stop them. And he knew exactly how to do it.

All he had to do was finish assembling the serum—and then take it.

Amy had her phone out and ready. The moment the plane's wheels touched the ground, she turned it on. It seemed to take forever before the home screen finally lit up.

And sure enough, there it was: a text message from Vesper One.

```
The winding trail now leads to Yale,
and four-oh-eight is oh so great!
Seventy-four and out the door.
You have three days—or someone pays.
```

Observe the tetrameter and perfect rhymes. I could have been a poet, don't you know it?

For weeks now, Amy and Dan had been gofers for the Vespers, a shadowy cabal and nemesis of the Cahill family for centuries. With the help of Dan's best friend, Atticus Rosenbloom, and his brother, Jake, Amy and Dan had traveled the globe stealing artifacts, manuscripts, artwork, even jewels, at the behest of the anonymous Vesper One.

Why? Because the Vespers were holding hostages. Seven people whom the Cahills cared about deeply, including two members of their immediate family — their guardians, Nellie Gomez and Fiske Cahill.

Vesper One had threatened to kill the hostages if Dan and Amy did not perform the specified tasks. This was the latest assignment: Go to Yale and steal — what?

Amy forwarded the text to Evan, who was overseeing the Cahill headquarters in Attleboro, Massachusetts. She added nothing further; Evan would know from the message where they were headed next.

Besides, she had absolutely no idea what to say to him.

"Hi, how's it going?" Utterly banal, given the circumstances.

"We need to talk." Like they could take the time for a cozy heart-to-heart in the midst of this Vesper-induced insanity.

"I have something I need to tell you. I know we're dating, but yesterday I kissed another boy."

Amy felt her face get hot. She didn't know if it was because she was mortified about even the idea of telling Evan . . . or if it was the thought of the kiss itself. She shut her eyes tightly, trying to blank out the memory of Jake's arms around her, the warmth of his lips . . .

STOP IT! Amy scolded herself inside her head. *Don't get distracted—you have to stay focused! Nellie, Fiske, Phoenix, all the rest—they need you!*

Maybe someday Amy would get to be a normal teenager with nothing to worry about except grades and friends and boys.

Maybe. But first, she had hostages to rescue.

Amy and Dan dashed through the terminal, with Jake and Atticus right on their heels. Amy couldn't remember the last time she had been able to *walk* through an airport.

She handed her phone to Dan so he could read Vesper One's text.

"Yale?" he panted. "What about the rest of it?"

"Don't know," she gasped back at him. "Guess we'll find out soon enough."

"Hey, wait up!" Fifty yards behind, Atticus was struggling with his jacket and backpack. Amy glanced over her shoulder and saw Jake turn around to help his brother by grabbing the pack. She plunged on, darting and weaving past knots of people.

They all caught up with each other at the taxi stand. The line wasn't long; they were able to get into the third cab. With Evan still on her mind, Amy took the front passenger seat so there wouldn't be any possibility of ending up thigh-to-thigh with Jake.

"Yale University," Amy said to the driver.

"Where is?" the driver asked.

"Connecticut. New Haven."

The driver shook his head. "No. No go that far."

Jake reached for the door handle. "Let's go," he said decisively. "No use wasting time — we'll find someone else to take us."

Who died and made him boss? Amy thought. She turned to the driver.

"We need to get to Yale," she said, "and we'll make it worth your while."

The man muttered to himself, then put some info into his GPS.

"Two hour there, two hour come back . . . I do it for six hundred," he said.

"Six hundred dollars?" Atticus yelped.

"Fine," Amy said.

The driver looked surprised; clearly he had picked an amount he thought they would never be able to afford.

"See money first," the driver said skeptically.

Amy took out her wallet, counted off six hundred-dollar bills, and flapped them at him. "There," she said. "Now can we *please* get going?"

As if the sight of the cash were a turbo-fuel injection, the driver gunned the engine and pulled out from the curb so fast that the tires squealed.

Amy raised her eyebrows at Jake. "Watch and learn," she said.

· He snorted, then swept his hand from his forehead toward her in an exaggerated mock bow. "As you wish, m'lady," he said.

Dan had put his backpack into the trunk of the cab but kept his laptop with him. Now he turned it on, clicked through to a search engine, and hesitated with his fingers over the keyboard.

"What should I type in?" he asked. "Yale, of course. And then what—four-oh-eight? Or maybe seventy-four?"

"No way!" Jake exclaimed.

Startled, Amy turned to see his eyes widening.

"Yale and four hundred eight? That has to be—" Jake stopped and shook his head.

Amy could see the shock in his expression.

"Amy, we can't—it's not—"

He took a breath. Then he looked at her pleadingly and said, "Please don't tell me we're going after the Voynich?"

CHAPTER 2

Toothpaste. Very important. That nasty feeling when you hadn't brushed in a while even had a name now: "biofilm." Yuck.

Enough of the idle thoughts. Hurry.

Some clothes (clean underwear also very important), phone charger, laptop and charger, camera, digital recorder . . . what else might be needed?

A couple of false IDs, just in case. And finally — most important — a piece of electronic equipment specially modified for the task. Can't just toss it in, gotta be gentle with it —

Was someone coming up the stairs? No, but they could be, any minute now. . . .

Get out, quick.

But quietly. Don't let the door slam.

Phoenix had never really been cold before.

He was cold to the very middle of every single one of his cells. His scalp and hair were like a cap knit of ice.

He couldn't see his face, but he knew that his lips were Crayola blue. Even his *toenails* were cold.

Never before had he shivered as long and hard as he was shivering now. And shivering was hard work. After a fitful night dozing against a tree trunk, Phoenix woke with deep aches in all his muscles.

As if being cold wasn't bad enough, now it hurt to shiver.

He was wandering through an endless forest where everything looked the same.

The trauma of the kidnapping, the confrontations with an enemy he couldn't even see, the physical and psychological deprivations of captivity, the escape and near drowning—his ordeal had drained his body and apparently his brain, too.

He just kept stumbling around in a stupor.

He tried to remember the books he had read about kids surviving in the wild. *Hatchet*—that kid had lived for weeks in the wilderness on his own, right?

But he had had—duh, a hatchet.

In frustration, Phoenix kicked at an old rotting stump. It cracked open a little, revealing an active colony of small white grubs.

Grubs. Bears ate grubs.

Humans did, too. He'd seen it on one of those crazy food shows.

Phoenix looked more closely into the crevice. There were dozens of grubs in the dead wood, pale and soft, wriggling and writhing and squirming. . . .

His stomach heaved at the sight of them.

He couldn't do it.

Turning away, he took a step and stumbled on the uneven ground. His reactions dulled by hunger and fatigue and cold, he couldn't catch himself, and fell to his knees. He felt tears coming into his eyes and let them roll down his cheeks unchecked.

At least they were warm.

Phoenix cried for a while. When he finally stopped and his vision cleared, he saw a slim stick in front of him. Almost a twig, really.

And he remembered something from another television program. On one of the nature channels. *Chimpanzees and termites . . .*

The edges of Phoenix's poor frozen brain started to thaw a little.

I have to get out of here and get help for the others. And I'll never be able to do that if I don't eat something.

Phoenix picked up the stick. He chewed one end of it until it was frayed, then fanned out the wood fibers. Now it looked like a broomstick for a very tiny witch.

He pushed the stick into the crack in the stump and waited a few moments. Slowly, carefully, he pulled it out.

There were three nice, fat grubs clinging to the frayed wood. *They'll taste like chicken,* he told himself.

Phoenix took a deep breath, closed his eyes, and opened his mouth.

Evan stared at the computer screen. *This can't be right.*

Some time ago, Evan had put out a call to Cahill operatives all over the world, asking for their help in identifying a mole in the network. *No one* was above suspicion. Not Amy, not Dan, not himself.

The results of the search were in, and Evan couldn't believe what he was seeing on the screen.

Something this big — I have to find a way to verify it. I need to be one hundred and ten percent sure before I tell Amy.

Evan shook off the shivers that were crawling down his spine, then shoved his ethical reservations firmly aside as he tapped into the suspect's computer.

Where to start? E-mails and documents would be the obvious choice. *Maybe too obvious . . . isn't that where you'd expect someone to start looking?*

Evan moused over the desktop icons.

Music . . . calendar . . . spreadsheets . . . photos . . .

Photos. *One picture is worth a thousand words?*

He clicked on the icon and, after only a few moments, found a password-protected file. It was quick work to figure out the password. *Tsk, tsk — shouldn't use the names of family members. Too easy.*

The file opened. Evan frowned.

There were several copies of a photo of Nellie — the one sent by the Vespers, in which she was thrusting a lizard toward the camera. The copies were identical.

Evan leaned closer to the screen. "What the heck?" he said aloud.

Identical, except for one thing: The lizards were different.

Green lizard. Brown lizard. Spotted, striped, bug-eyed . . . There was no question about it: The photos had been manipulated. The lizard in the original photo had been swapped out for different ones. The last four photos showed the same lizard altered slightly for size and position.

A tegu lizard, from Argentina. That's what she said.

Evan sat back and gulped for air, trying to settle the sick feeling that was roiling his stomach.

South America — where Ian was. She was trying to make us think it was him.

She, meaning Sinead.

Amy's best friend.

Who knew everything — *everything* — about the Cahill operation. The damage she could do —

Evan was on his feet and headed for the door. He ran up the stairs and down a hallway, shouldered open a door, and hit the light switch.

Drawers gaping, closet ajar, clothes discarded on the floor — all the signs of a hasty exit.

He was too late.

Sinead was gone.

Evan spun around wildly and crashed into the door frame in his haste to get back to the comm center.

He had to tell Amy that Sinead was the mole. If Sinead got to her first . . . Evan's heart was pounding.

Amy could be in terrible danger.

CHAPTER 3

Dan, Amy, and Atticus all stared at Jake.

"What the heck is the Voynich?" Dan asked, followed immediately by, "What's the four-oh-eight?" from Amy.

"It's an old manuscript," Jake answered, "kept by the Beinecke Library at Yale. In their collection, the Voynich is manuscript number four hundred eight. But I'm not sure what the seventy-four means."

"How do you know all that?" Atticus asked.

Jake slumped against the seat back. "Mom," he said quietly.

"Your mom had something to do with the Voynich?" Amy asked.

Jake scowled at her. *Why does she have to question everything I say?*

"That was her field," he said with exaggerated patience. "Mostly the ancient world, but sometimes medieval, too. She liked old stuff. Is that okay with you?"

Amy held her hands up in mock surrender. "Sorry for asking," she said.

Jake turned back to the group and said, "Get comfy, everyone. This is a long story.

"Mom always had a lot of different projects going," Jake said. "But for years, no matter what else she was working on, she always went back to the Voynich. She used to talk to me about it."

"Huh," Atticus said. "She never told me about it."

Jake was silent for a moment. "When she first got into it, you were really little," he said. "And then — well, it was sort of our thing. Like, special, between the two of us." Pause. "I think she was trying to make sure I knew it didn't matter that she wasn't my birth mom. . . ."

His voice trailed off.

Astrid had been his stepmother. His own mother — his dad's first wife — had passed away when Jake was only a year old. His dad had remarried two years later; Astrid was the only mom he had ever really known.

It had been more than a year since her death. The pain was duller now, but it was still there, and he was pretty sure it always would be.

"Okay," Atticus said. "That's cool."

Jake nodded gratefully at his brother, then took the laptop from Dan.

"So, the Voynich," Jake said. "It's a whole book — I can't remember exactly, but it's over two hundred pages long. And it's really old."

"How old?" Amy asked.

"They weren't sure, for a long time," Jake said. "This bookseller named Voynich — that's where it got its name—he found it in an old monastery in Italy. In 1912, I think. And he bought it from the monks. Ever since then, there have been all these theories. Some people thought it was from the thirteenth century, or it was from the eighteenth, or it was modern, a forgery. Then a few years ago, the Beinecke had it carbon-dated. Both the pages and the ink are fifteenth century, which proves—"

"That it isn't a forgery," Dan said.

"No, not exactly," Jake said. "What it proves is that it's a medieval document. I mean, a really determined forger could get really old vellum and really old ink, but they're pretty sure that's not what happened."

"So what kind of document is it?" Amy asked. "What does it say?"

Jake snorted. "That," he said, "is the problem."

Jake went on to explain that the Voynich was written in an unknown language—one never seen before.

"And nobody's been able to figure it out," he said.

He started clicking on the laptop. "Yale gets so many requests to see the manuscript that they couldn't keep up with all of them," he said. "So they finally digitized the whole thing, and now anyone who wants to study it can look at the pages online."

A few clicks, and he had a digital image of one of the pages from the Voynich.

"Look," he said. He turned the screen around so they could all see it.

"Is it in code?" Dan asked. "It looks like something you could figure out. I mean, not *you* you, but somebody."

"That's what everybody thinks when they first see it," Jake said. "But hundreds of people have tried—maybe thousands. Even the government got into it. You know the guys who broke the Japanese and German codes during World War II? They worked on it for *years* and got nothing."

"Wow," Amy said. "That's amazing."

Jake glanced at her quickly. She was looking at the screen, not at him, and there didn't seem to be any edge to her voice.

Girls. The oldest mystery in the universe. Amy was acting like their kiss had never happened. *It wasn't just me,* Jake thought. *She definitely kissed me back.*

"What are the pictures of?" Dan asked.

"Three kinds of illustrations," Jake answered. *Click*— "Botanical drawings" — *click click*— "astronomical charts" — *click click* — "and these weird ones. Mom always called them the plumbing pictures."

"Hello!" Dan said.

The "plumbing pictures" showed water flowing through pipes, basins, and aqueducts. In almost all of them, there were naked women swimming.

Atticus nudged Dan and they both giggled.

"Oh, please," Amy said. Jake could see that she was a little embarrassed. She changed the subject. "What about the botanical drawings? Wouldn't they give a clue to where the book was written, or what it's about?"

"You'd think so," Jake said. "But the plants aren't from real life. I mean, they think they've identified a couple of them, but even those have parts that aren't real."

Jake sighed. "All kinds of people have tried to figure it out. Historians, of course, like Mom. But also botanists, astronomers, linguists, mathematicians, philosophers, theologians—"

"Plumbers?" Dan said with a snicker.

Jake grinned. "Some scholars have spent their whole lives working on it," he said. "And you wouldn't believe the theories they come up with."

"Like what?" Atticus asked.

"Aliens," Jake said. "And angels. That's just two of them."

"You can't be serious," Amy said.

"I'm not, but *they* are," Jake said. "And even some of the more credible theories are pretty out-there. Like, it's an old form of Ukrainian, but you're only supposed to read every fifth letter."

Dan had sobered up now that the subject was not naked women. "What about the seventy-four?" he asked. "Do you think that means we're supposed to steal page seventy-four?"

"Or maybe, the first seventy-four pages?" Amy guessed.

"But that's not the most important question, not really," Atticus said. "The question is, why do the Vespers want it? If they can't read it, it's no use to them."

Jake frowned, thinking hard. "I get what you're saying," he said slowly. "If the Vespers are smart enough to read the Voynich, we're *really* in trouble."

They had been making decent progress from the airport through the borough of Queens, in taxi mode: mad spurts of shouldering through traffic alternating with a sulky crawl. Now, as they drove onto the Whitestone Bridge, the driver whistled through his teeth. "Look like trouble here," he said.

A police car was parked across the lanes. An officer stood facing them, arm up, palm flat, in the classic "halt" stance. The taxi stopped, and within seconds, the bridge entrance behind them became a giant parking lot packed with cars.

Beyond the cop, the last of the cars that had been allowed through disappeared from sight. The bridge's roadway was now completely clear.

"What's going on?" Dan asked from the back.

"There's a motorcycle—" Amy said. "No, wait, it's like a motorcade, sort of."

Three SUVs with motorcycles front and rear were coming toward them on the wrong side of the road. *Celebrity?* Amy thought. *Or maybe some politician.*

As if he could hear her thoughts, Dan said, "Must be somebody pretty important to stop a whole bridge's worth of traffic."

Then he gasped, and the heads of the other three swiveled to stare at him.

It was as if all four of them had the same thought at the same moment.

Who had that kind of power?

The Vespers!

"Move!" Amy said urgently.

They scrambled out of the car. The taxi driver began yelling at them.

"Hey! Where you going? You say Connettytuck, I taking you there!" He got out, too, and grabbed Dan's arm.

"My backpack!" Dan said. "The trunk, open the trunk!"

He twisted out of the driver's grasp, leaned inside the open door, and groped around for the trunk release. He hit the buttons for the warning lights and the gas cap before he found the right one, the driver scolding him in a language he didn't understand.

"Dan, leave it!" Amy said. "We have to get out of here!" But Dan ran to the back of the taxi and grabbed the pack.

The motorcycle pulled over. The lead SUV made a U-turn and stopped near the police car. The driver-side door opened.

"RUN!" Amy yelled. "If we get separated, meet up at Yale!"

She glanced around wildly. They were on a bridge, with only two choices: forward or back. And forward was toward the SUVs.

Which meant they had *no* choice. Two minus one equals zero: Vesper math.

Amy turned and started running back the way they had come.

CHAPTER 4

A voice called out, "Amy!"

It wasn't the boys, they were still with her, but Amy knew that her instincts had been right: It was someone who knew they'd be here, on their way to Yale. . . .

Dodging between the cars as fast as she could, Amy felt bewilderment mixed with fear. *This is crazy! Vesper One* needs *us for this mission — why would he send people to stop us?*

"Amy! Amy Cahill!"

A small part of her brain tried to free itself from the panic and think rationally. *I know that voice — who —*

"AMY! STOP! STOP, IT'S ME, SINEAD!"

Amy hugged Sinead, tears of relief in her eyes. "I was never so glad to see anyone in my whole life," Amy said.

They walked back to the SUV. Sinead signaled the rest of the motorcade, and they departed.

"Who are they?" Amy asked.

"Private security firm," Sinead said. "Mostly

ex-SWAT or Navy SEALs. And our Lucian friends got in touch with the mayor, who helped out with the traffic."

Amy smiled in gratitude. "But why didn't you call and tell me you were coming?"

"It's Yale, right?" Sinead said briskly. "Come on, we better get going." She threw her arm around Amy's shoulders. "It's great to be together again!"

"Ditto," Amy said, and the thought that Sinead hadn't answered the question faded from her mind.

It had almost been like a game.

A chess match that she had played perfectly, each move with patience and purpose. Sinead felt a tremendous amount of satisfaction thinking about the months that had gone by without Amy suspecting a thing.

Now it was time for the end game, just three moves left. First, get the serum formula. Second, present it with a flourish to Vesper One, whose gratitude would surely be boundless. And third, the most important, reunite with Ned and Ted to give them the serum.

The Starlings had given up all claim to the serum when the Clue hunt ended. But back then, the doctors still seemed to have plenty of strategies available in their attempts to cure Ted's blindness and Ned's headaches.

It had been more than two years now. Nothing had worked, and they were out of options. Sinead was desperate. The serum had to be the answer; it would succeed where the doctors had failed.

As for her friendship with Amy . . . Sinead felt a twinge, a vibration of regret that she tamped instantly.

My family. My brothers. That's what matters.

Sinead's hand slid to her pocket. She fingered the barrel of her new gun with both pride and tenderness.

Are you the best ickle gun in the world? Yes you are, oh, yes you are. . . .

A SwissMiniGun. The world's smallest handgun, just two inches long. Sinead had briefly considered the eighteen-karat-gold, diamond-studded version—which cost more than forty thousand dollars—but opted in the end for the more practical stainless-steel model.

Removed from the holster, the gun could actually be hidden in the palm of her hand, and it sounded pretty much like a cap gun when it was fired. The bullets were not much bigger than pinheads—dollhouse bullets that looked like they couldn't hurt a flea.

Sinead found this vaguely comforting, because the honest truth was that she didn't want to hurt Amy. *Only if I have to . . .*

The bullets were real enough, though, and exited the barrel at three hundred miles per hour. At point-blank range, they could penetrate human flesh and do plenty of damage to a vital organ or a major artery.

Normally, getting that close to an adversary would be a tricky task. But not in this case.

After all, she and Amy were best friends.

"It's not looking good," Sinead said.

She wasn't talking about the road, which was blissfully empty for now, all the traffic ahead of them cleared by her stunt on the bridge.

She was talking about the hostages.

"We enhanced the last video feed so we could get a good look at everyone. Alistair is the worst off. I hate to say this, but he looks really awful. His eyes — I don't know quite how to put it. It's like he's given up already."

Amy turned to meet Dan's gaze and saw her own worry reflected in his expression. Alistair Oh was not the oldest hostage — Fiske Cahill was a few years older — but Fiske was in many ways like his sister Grace, Amy and Dan's grandmother. Both seemed to have a thin core of steel running through them.

Alistair, on the other hand, had shuttled back and forth between sympathy and nefariousness, alternately helping and hurting the Cahills. Although he had finally ended up on their side for good, his ambivalence was perhaps a symptom of a deeper weakness. The kidnapping and captivity seemed to be sapping not only his physical strength, but his will to live as well.

Amy swallowed and forced out the next words. "Anything more about — about Phoenix?"

Sinead shook her head. Silence all around.

Phoenix, only twelve years old . . . It wasn't like Amy could have done anything to prevent his death. But that knowledge didn't help. Wretched. And *like* retching, that was how it made her feel.

For a while Amy heard nothing but the muted sounds of traffic through what she guessed was the bulletproof glass of the car's windows.

"Amy."

Sinead had her eyes on the road, and Amy could tell that whatever was coming, it was serious.

"No one wants to talk about this, but we have to," Sinead said. She glanced back at Dan.

Without asking, Amy knew what Sinead meant.

The serum.

The main reason that the Vespers were targeting the Cahills was a formula Gideon Cahill had invented in the sixteenth century. If all of its ingredients were precisely and painstakingly measured and mixed, the result would be a serum that gave its imbibers abilities and talents that made them superior to most of the human race.

The thirty-nine components of the serum had been discovered, and Dan had memorized the exact formula before it was destroyed.

"The one thing that could defeat them once and for all," Sinead said. "I'm not saying we should use it, but I *am* saying that we need to think about it."

"I've been—" Dan started to speak, but cut himself off.

Amy looked at him sharply. "You've been what?"

Dan shifted in his seat. "I've been—I mean, I have

been thinking about it," he said. "I can't help it, it's stuck there in my brain."

"Exactly my point," Sinead said. "Dan has the formula in his head. No one else knows it. On the one hand, that makes it safe from the Vespers. But on the other hand, it means none of us can get at it, either."

"And why would we need to?" Amy demanded. "We're not going to use it. Not ever. It's way too much power for any one person."

"I know," Sinead said, "but supposing — worst-case scenario here — supposing the Vespers get hold of Dan somehow. And they torture him, and he gives up the formula —"

"You think — Are you crazy?!" Dan spluttered indignantly. "They could pull out every one of my fingernails — I'd never give it up!"

"Okay, okay," Sinead said. "I said, worst-case scenario."

"Besides," Atticus piped up, "I know you'd never give it up willingly, but what if they gave you truth serum or something?"

"Yeah, that's what I meant." Sinead flashed a grateful glance in the mirror at Atticus. "And then — then something terrible happens to Dan, and now *they're* the only ones who have it."

"So what are you saying?" Amy said. She couldn't keep the testiness out of her voice. She hated the serum and everything it stood for. Not for the first time, she wished there was a way to go into Dan's brain and vacuum out the cells that held the formula.

"We need to store it somewhere," Sinead said. "Somewhere really secure. Where we could get to it but no one else could."

"Fort Knox, maybe?" A lame response. Amy knew that sarcasm was not one of her strong points.

"Amy, please. Listen to what I'm saying."

Sinead's voice was steady. *She's being patient with me even though I'm hassling her,* Amy thought, and felt a wave of warmth: It was so good to be with a girlfriend again after all the hours with just the boys.

"I was thinking of a password-protected file," Sinead went on. "Maybe on a secure cell phone."

"And who would have access to the password?"

"Your call," Sinead said immediately. "I mean, it would be good if more than one person had it, in case of—of Vesper interference. But it would be up to you, whoever you think you could trust."

Amy stared out the window for a long time. The miles rolled by in silence.

She glanced behind her once and saw that both Jake and Atticus were dozing off, Atticus with his head lolling forward, Jake leaning against the window with his mouth partly open. He looked cute in that awkward pose, maybe even cuter because of it.

But Dan was awake and staring out the window, too. Amy could tell from his solemn expression that his brain felt like hers did: crowded with too many thoughts, too few of them pleasant.

Who can I trust one hundred percent, besides Dan?

Fiske and Nellie. *Currently unavailable,* she thought grimly.

With a stab of pain in her gut, she thought of Erasmus. *He would have been perfect for this.*

Amy could see water to her right now, an inlet of the Long Island Sound, and soon after that, they took the exit for Yale.

As they drove onto the campus, Sinead broke the silence. "One other thing," she said. "It's too much pressure for one person." She jerked her chin toward the backseat. "He shouldn't be carrying that burden alone. As it is now, any decision about the serum, ultimately he has to make it all by himself. This way, other people would be sharing the load."

"It's not a problem," Dan said quickly. "I can handle it."

"No one's saying you can't," Amy said. "I mean, it's obvious — you've been handling it all this time. But Sinead's right. Things are different now that the Vespers are active."

"Active" — now there's a euphemism for you.

Who was left?

Sinead, of course. Amy felt relief coursing through her. *Weird that I didn't think of her right away. She'd take a bullet for me. What would I do without her?*

"Okay," she said. She nodded at Sinead. "Let's do it. As soon as we get to Yale."

CHAPTER 5

As Sinead searched for a parking spot, Amy saw that Yale looked exactly like she'd imagined it would, autumn sunlight warming the pale honey-colored stone buildings, students everywhere. It was a New England postcard come to life. *I bet the libraries here are awesome,* she thought.

Sinead eased the SUV into a space on a side street that led to the Beinecke Library. Amy took out her phone slowly, still thinking. She tapped idly at the screen to bring up her messages, then frowned.

"That's strange," she said.

"What's wrong?" Sinead asked.

"Error message. No connection."

"Mine, too," Dan said from the back.

"Want me to have a look?" Sinead asked.

Amy reached for the door handle. "Maybe it would be better outside the car."

"Wait," Sinead said. "Let me see it first."

Amy caught it then — the strained, overeager tone of Sinead's voice. Her brain turned over slowly: *Why does*

Sinead want to get her hands on my phone?

Amy got out of the car and looked at her phone. She was getting a signal now. Sinead jumped out of the driver's side and rushed around the front of the car.

"I can fix it!" Sinead shouted and snatched at the phone. She knocked it out of Amy's hand, and it fell to the ground.

But Amy had already seen the first of several text messages from Evan.

URGENT—SINEAD MOLE.

Reeling.

That's what it said in books: "So-and-so reeled at the news." Now Amy knew what it felt like.

Her stomach reeled—churning and roiling with that about-to-be-sick feeling. Her vision reeled, the world spinning and swirling in maniacal loops of color. And her brain reeled, the thoughts careening around and smashing into each other.

Amy raised her eyes slowly to meet Sinead's. Evan hadn't gotten it wrong: The bitterness in Sinead's eyes was so sharp that Amy could almost taste it.

"Why?" Amy asked, her voice barely more than a squeak.

Jake started to get out of the car, but Amy raised her hand in a fierce gesture to stop him.

"You don't have a clue, do you?" Sinead said. Her voice was ice-cold and hot with anger at the same time.

It was like a different person speaking — someone Amy didn't know. "My brothers. They'll never be the same."

Ted, blind. Ned, incapacitated by terrible headaches for which doctors could find neither cause nor cure. Their injuries had occurred near the very start of the hunt for the 39 Clues.

"If it weren't for Grace's stupid competition, nothing would have happened to them. I hate the Cahills. Everything about them, everything they stand for. And that includes you."

Amy's stomach still felt utterly unreliable. She swallowed hard. "So you — you're with *them* now?"

Sinead nodded. "The Vespers won't stop at anything. They're going to be the most powerful people on the planet. And with all that money and power, they might be able to help Ned and Ted."

"But Ted is one of the hostages!" Amy protested. "How could you —"

For the first time, Sinead seemed to waver a little. "He's not going to be harmed. And once I explain everything to him, he'll understand."

Amy's mind was still trying to get hold of the idea that their friendship for the past two years was a complete sham. The very ground she stood on felt shaky at the thought. *How can I ever trust my own judgment again?*

Sinead was still speaking. "We're triplets," she said, "and you can't possibly imagine what that means. Whatever you feel for Dan, it's *nothing*, not a rat's ass compared to —"

Without even thinking about it, Amy kicked out as hard as she could, striking Sinead on her left side.

Sinead's legs buckled momentarily but she regained her balance, then turned and ran.

Amy was caught off guard; she had expected Sinead to fight back. In the second it took her to adjust and start running, Sinead got a good head start.

Faster! Amy's feet pounded hard on the pavement, keeping time with her throbbing pulse. She heard voices and the sound of car doors slamming as the three boys joined in the chase well behind her.

Then Sinead took a sharp left turn between two buildings. Amy saw her just in time and made the turn herself. She tried to yell to let the boys know, but what came out was a breathless, jagged noise that didn't make sense even to her.

She found herself running down a narrow alley that led to a little courtyard with wrought-iron patio furniture. A dense bed of ivy grew along the base of the back wall, which was ten feet high and topped with a row of ornate iron spikes. No sound of the boys behind her; they must have missed the turnoff.

Sinead spun around to face Amy. Sinead raised one arm; she seemed to be holding something very small between her thumb and forefinger.

"It's a gun," Sinead said menacingly. "Don't come any closer." She raised her voice to a near-scream. "Stay right where you are or I'll shoot!"

Amy wasn't sure whether to laugh or cry — to laugh

at Sinead's straight-from-Hollywood-cliché line or to cry because her best friend was pointing a gun at her. *At least, she seems to think it's a gun. . . .*

"A gun—yeah, right," Amy said, trying to make her voice sound tough. "An invisible gun? Or maybe an imaginary one?"

"It's a SwissMiniGun," Sinead said. "The smallest in the world. Real bullets."

"There's no gun that small," Amy said.

"Oh, yeah? Want to find out?" Sinead taunted.

If I can get close enough, Amy thought, *maybe I can pin her to the wall, keep her there until the boys show up.* She took a slow, cautious step toward Sinead, who backed up a corresponding step. They continued this dance until Sinead was standing in the ivy with nowhere to go.

"Don't come any closer!" Sinead screeched.

Amy took a breath to try to keep any tremor out of her voice. "I don't believe it's a gun," she said. "You're gonna have to prove it to me."

She took one more step.

With a roar, Sinead lunged forward, grabbed Amy's arm, and shoved something against her neck.

Instantly, instinctively, Amy twisted her head and body. Then—*BANG!*

CHAPTER 6

Am I dead?

The inside of Amy's head was shuddering violently, as if it held a giant gong that had just been struck full force.

My ear — my right ear — oh, my God, it really WAS a gun — I can't believe — what's wrong with my ear?

Meanwhile, Sinead was attempting to reposition the gun for another shot; not surprisingly, a delicate and fiddly operation. Amy yelled, her own voice sounding dull through the gonging in her brain. She wrenched her arm free and went into kickboxing mode.

For an agonizing second, Amy stood frozen. Still dizzy and disoriented, was she really going to have to engage in a one-on-one, full-contact, bare-knuckle fight? Despite the months of kickboxing lessons with Sensei Takamoto, she had never truly imagined what it would be like to attack another human being.

Then her vision cleared and her gaze landed on the gun. Sinead had her finger on the tiny trigger.

It was amazing how fast Amy's self-defense

mechanism kicked in. She went straight to her best move, spinning to her right and using the one-two of centrifugal force and thrust to connect with Sinead's hand.

Solid contact: A tiny object flew through the air and fell into the ivy.

"NO!" Sinead shouted. She dropped to her knees, scrabbling through the ivy vines in a desperate search.

Amy had seen the gun fall to her right; Sinead was looking in the wrong place. *Go for it! NOW!*

Another solid hit: Sinead plowed into a planter, crushing a geranium and scattering its scarlet petals. But she was on her feet again in the next second. Abandoning all of Sensei's dictates, she launched herself at Amy, knocked her to the ground, and started in on a good old-fashioned hair-pulling, nail-clawing catfight, complete with screeches.

It was absurd: Amy wanted to cry out, "No, no! This is NOT what we were taught!" But she was too busy trying to keep Sinead's claws out of her eyes.

Sinead was on top, and she was bigger and stronger than Amy. One of Amy's arms was pinned under Sinead's knee. Her left hand yanked at Amy's hair while her right went for a stranglehold to the throat.

Amy tried to smash Sinead's nose with a flat palm but couldn't generate any real force. All she did was shove Sinead's face back a few inches. Sinead was bearing down as hard as she could on Amy's throat. Struggling vainly, her airway closing off,

Amy was starting to see stars.

Sinead had a death grip, with most of her weight behind it. Her eyes glittered with the knowledge that she had a clear edge in the fight.

As strangled, choking sounds came from her throat, Amy did the only thing she could think of: She used her remaining air to hock a big gob of spit into Sinead's face.

"AARGH!"

Sinead loosened her grip for just a moment, but it was long enough. Amy head-butted her squarely in the nose. Sinead's head snapped back, and blood poured from her nostrils. As Sinead clapped her hands to her face in agony, Amy rolled out from under.

For a few moments she saw red—literally, as the capillaries in her eyes were reinfused with blood. She heard the sound before she saw the sight: Sinead, one hand to her nose, running back up the alley.

"HEY!" Jake's voice. "What the—OOF!"

Sinead had barreled him out of the way.

"Stop her!" Amy tried to shout, but what came out was barely above a whisper.

Jake rushed into the courtyard to see Amy on her knees in the ivy. It was too late to go after Sinead.

"What happened? Are you okay?" Jake asked.

No. I'm not okay. I might never be okay again. But she nodded mutely.

"What happened to your neck?" he said, crouching next to her.

Amy became aware of a sore spot on the side of her neck that seemed to be something apart from the bruises caused by Sinead's grip.

"Hold still," he said and touched the spot gingerly. He frowned and looked at his fingertips, which were dusted with a gray substance.

"Argahgargah," she said, then cleared her throat twice and still the words came out raspy. "That must be, like, gunshot residue."

"She had a GUN!?" Jake looked stricken.

Her ear still ringing, Amy slumped against the wall. She felt something under her hand and picked it up.

"What is it?" Jake was kneeling beside her.

She held out her hand, palm outstretched. In it was the smallest gun either of them had ever seen.

The barrel was still warm.

Back at the car, Amy was relieved to find that while the hearing in her right ear was a little woolly, the ringing sound had faded. And the powder burn on her neck didn't seem to be serious. She told the boys what had transpired, surprised by how calm her voice was. For now, she had to relate just the facts. *If I think about anything else, I'll probably start crying.*

"Wow," Dan said, examining the gun. "What do you bet it was an Ekat who came up with this?"

"We found something under the dashboard," Atticus said. He held out an electronic device. "It's a signal blocker. She didn't want us getting any messages."

Silence, while each of them considered the implications of having had a mole in their midst for so long.

"She must know where the hostages are," Amy said. The thought made her so angry that her voice shook.

"And her brother is one of them!" Atticus said. "Do you think he's in on it?"

Amy shook her head. "He's not. She told me."

"But she's letting them keep him locked up!" Atticus was incredulous. He looked at Jake. "And I thought *you* were a pain sometimes."

"Gee, thanks, bro," Jake said in mock gratitude.

Just then Amy's phone beeped with a text:

I'm here at Yale—where are you?

It was from Evan.

Evan was hurrying toward them when he caught sight of Amy and stopped short, obviously aghast. For a moment, Amy was actually glad she looked so awful; she had been anxious about how he would greet her. With a hug, or even a kiss?

So what? That's what boyfriends do, and he's my boyfriend. Why should I care what—what Jake thinks?

"I'm fine," she said to forestall his worry. "It was Sinead."

Evan looked startled, then miserable. He touched

her arm hesitantly. "It's my fault," he said. "I didn't catch on to her fast enough. And then I kept trying to text you—"

"It was not your fault!" Amy snapped. "She almost talked us into giving up the serum formula—if it hadn't been for you, we might have done it! The worst of it is, she got away."

"As long as you're okay," Evan said. "But you had her, four against one—how did you lose her?"

"Look," Jake said, his voice edged with annoyance. "You weren't there—you didn't see how it went down."

Evan bristled. "You're right, I wasn't there, so I want to know—"

"Evan—I mean, um, Jake"—Amy felt the beginnings of a mild panic—"both of you—this is not helping!"

Both of the older boys had the grace to look sheepish. Amy took a deep breath and exhaled slowly.

"Can we start over? Evan, this is Jake and Atticus. Jake and Atticus, meet Evan."

It was Atticus who broke the tension.

"Hey, Evan, nice to finally meet you," he said.

Amy could have hugged him. "Let's all find somewhere to sit down," she suggested. "And then we'll get you caught up, Jake—I mean, Evan."

She wanted to bite her tongue off.

Dan snickered. "Oops," he said. "Why don't you just call them both Jakevan—wouldn't that be easier?"

If looks could kill, Dan would have been six feet under.

What's eating her?

Evan wondered if it had anything to do with him. Then he felt ashamed. *Sheesh, give the girl a break.*

Amy had marched off to find a restroom. When she came back, she looked more herself—face washed, hair brushed, a fresh T-shirt. Evan's spirits rose at the sight of her.

They found a bench outside the library.

"Okay, I've had a chance to think about this," Amy said. "I'm going to lay it out now, and you can let me know what you think."

Nods all around.

"First, we'll need to send an urgent bulletin about Sinead. That's you, Evan. A message to the entire Cahill network to keep their eyes peeled for her."

"What should they do if they spot her?" Evan asked.

"Keep her locked down until we can get her to reveal the location of the hostages. Otherwise, any sightings should be reported so you can coordinate the hunt."

"Got it," Evan said. He was impressed by her businesslike tone, which made him feel proud. He smiled at her.

She nodded, but didn't smile back.

"Next. This one's on me." Amy hesitated for a moment; whatever was coming, it wasn't pleasant. "I have to call Ian and apologize. For thinking he was the mole all this time."

"Not your fault," Dan said. "It was obviously Sinead feeding you bad info."

"Garbage in, garbage out," Atticus agreed.

"Maybe not my fault," Amy said, "but still my responsibility."

Now she raised her chin toward the building in front of them. "After that, we need a plan for the Voynich," she said. "Sinead has been a major distraction. We have to get back on track."

"We need to talk about this," Jake said. "Do we have to steal it?"

"Of course we have to steal it," Evan said. "Like everything else so far — why should this be any different?" *Funny how things change,* he thought. *Just a few weeks ago I'd have been asking the same question. . . .*

Amy held up her hand. "We can discuss that in a minute," she said. "Let me get through the list first." Pause. "Once I get things straightened out with Ian, I want him to work with you, Evan, on finding the hostages. Dan and I have to keep playing Vesper One's game — it's too risky not to. But I don't trust him — "

"You think?" Dan said in disgust.

" — so I want us focusing on rescue as much as on release. Whatever you need, whatever it takes."

Evan didn't respond right away. He made eye contact with Amy.

"Can I talk to you for a second?" he said quietly.

He saw a flicker of uncertainty in her eyes, but then she blinked it away. She stood and walked away from the bench, around the corner of a retaining wall, where they had a little privacy.

Amy crossed her arms, looking almost defensive; Evan could tell that she was not in girlfriend mode. He wanted to touch her, but instead put a hand on the wall and leaned against it. Close to her, but not touching.

No use beating around the bush. "I don't want to go back to Attleboro," he said. "I want to stay here with you."

"Not an option," she said immediately. "We need someone at the comm center and on the computers. You're the only one who can do it."

He sighed. "I knew you'd say that," he said. "I guess—I just wanted you to know that I'd rather be with you. I miss you."

Say it, he begged silently, *say you miss me, too.*

Amy was staring at the ground. "I know," she whispered.

Then she straightened up and looked at him with an expression of—apology? Regret? Maybe even guilt? Why wouldn't she tell him what she was thinking?

"Evan, I can't . . . I'm sorry. We have work to do." She touched his arm briefly, then walked back to the others.

As they rejoined the group, Evan saw Jake give him a long, cool stare. Evan's stomach double-clutched.

Does he—Is Amy—

He tried to force his thoughts in a different direction. *Don't think about it. It's not important, not right now.*

But another part of him wanted to shout, *Yes, it is! It's important to ME!*

Evan jammed his hands into his pockets. His shoulders hunched, he watched her out of the corner of his eye.

I can wait, he thought. *Until this craziness ends. And then we can talk, and everything will be okay.*

Maybe it wasn't true. But for now, it wasn't false, either.

He'd take those odds. She was worth it.

"Ian, it's Amy. I'm here with Dan. And Jake and Atticus."

A brief silence. Then, "Hello."

Never had that word sounded less welcoming. Amy sighed—he wasn't going to make this easy. And she had the added pressure of making this call with an audience: The phone was on speaker, so the four boys with her could hear everything.

"Evan found out—Sinead is the mole." She could almost hear the click of a door closing on her emotions, blocking out the pain that went with those words. *Focus,* she told herself firmly.

No response from Ian.

"Ian, I'm sorry."

Still no response.

"Look, I know we screwed up big-time."

Finally: "That would seem to be an understatement of laughable proportions," he said.

Followed by silence again.

Amy gritted her teeth. "Ian, come on. I'll say it

again: I'm really, really sorry. What do you want me to do, beg?"

"As a matter of fact, yes," Ian said.

Jake bristled. "Hey, where do you get off?"

Amy scowled at him. "I don't need your help, and besides, you're just going to make him madder."

"You don't even know him," Evan protested to Jake. "He's okay, he's just pissed off right now. Amy, if you want, I can try—"

Amy glared at the two of them. "Would you both please shut up? Ian—" She paused, trying to figure out a way to break through to him. *Maybe if I ask a question . . .* "Is there any way I can make this right?"

Ian cleared his throat. "I would have thought you would have given me the benefit of the doubt," he said, his accent more clipped than she had ever heard before. "After all, we do have a considerable history together."

Amy felt her face go pink. A couple of years ago, she had had a crush on Ian, which, it turned out, had been mutual. Was that what he was referring to? *I hope not—I'm already all mixed up when it comes to boys!*

The pain of Sinead's betrayal came back in full force. Like most girls and women, Amy confided in her female friends, and just yesterday she had drafted an e-mail to Sinead about kissing Jake. She hadn't had a chance to send it, and now she never would.

Amy forced herself to concentrate. "I know that. But think about it, Ian—the recent history with you has been — well, worrying. You left Attleboro without telling anyone where you were going, and no one could get in touch with you. Then when you got back, you wouldn't tell Evan where you'd been. We didn't want to think the worst, but can you see how it looked?"

Another silence, but somehow this one seemed less frosty.

"I see your point," he said. "But the phrase *benefit of the doubt* means that one holds off doubting and gives the subject time to explain. Or whatever."

"You're right," she said, "and I'm sorry. Really I am. If you're willing to explain now, I'm ready. Late to the party is better than — than missing the boat entirely, right?"

A pause. Then, "I shall plan a party on the *Force*."

"The *Force* — you mean, your yacht?" Amy was startled by the sudden change in subject.

He snorted. "Yes, and you can arrive late, thus rescuing you from that appalling mixed metaphor."

Amy laughed, partly at his joke and partly from relief; her approach seemed to be working. *And now for a little ego stroking . . .*

"Okay, can we talk about what you've been up to? The rest of you, listen up. Whatever Ian has to say, I'm sure it's important."

"Amy. Please. I'm going to explain everything whether or not you flatter me, so you needn't bother."

Amy blushed again. "Okay, you got me. But I meant it, too. Go ahead."

CHAPTER 7

Ian's explanation was concise and efficient. He told them that his mother Isabel's charity, AWW, was highly suspect. She appeared to be using it as a cover, traveling all over the world.

"She's been to Alaska, Istanbul, Quito in Ecuador—"

"Wait. Ian, this is Dan. You said she's using the charity as a cover—for what?"

"Ah. That I have not yet been able to deduce. The locations seem quite random. If there is anything connecting them, I do not know what it is. Other than poor people, which gives AWW a reason to be there." Pause. "It seems there are poor people everywhere."

Amy noticed that there was no disdain in his voice, as there might have been a couple of years ago.

"Ian, would you send me the list of where she's been, and copy it to Attleboro? Maybe if all of us work on it, we can figure something out."

"What is it you Americans say — 'Hey okay'?"

Atticus giggled. "'A-okay,'" he said.

"Yes. Well. You knew what I meant." Ian seemed

back to his usual self now, unflappable and confident-borderline-arrogant.

Amy discussed with him the next step: working with Evan to find the hostages. Ian agreed readily. As they ended the call, Amy felt a little better. That, at least, had gone fairly well.

Evan stood up. "Guess I better get going," he said reluctantly. He fist-bumped Dan and nodded at Jake and Atticus. Then he turned to Amy.

The look in his eyes—equal parts anxious and hopeful—made her feel terrible again. She hugged him quickly, knowing that Jake was right there watching.

The exterior of the Beinecke resembled a pane of giant postage stamps made of marble, its lines clean and modern. It did not look like a building that held rare books. It looked more like a futuristic art museum, or perhaps an experimental cloning facility.

As the four teens entered through the glass doors, they could see a uniformed security guard at the front desk. Clearly this was no ordinary library.

Amy approached the desk first and introduced the group as homeschoolers on a field trip. "We're studying the Renaissance," she said brightly. She found it a little scary to consider how practiced she had become at lying to strangers. "And we know that the Beinecke has a lot of medieval manuscripts, so we were wondering—"

"The Voynich!" Atticus came in right on cue,

bouncing a little in excitement. "Amy, ask about the Voynich!"

"Okay, okay!" she said, laughing a little, and turned back to the guard. "He's pretty excited—we've been learning a lot about it."

Not lying there.

The guard didn't smile, but his face was kind. "The Voynich is kept in secure storage," he said. "It's not on display for the general public."

Amy's face fell. (That, too, was genuine.) "They don't bring it out, not ever?"

"Requests have to be submitted in advance, in writing," he said. "And even if you do that, I should warn you that very few requests are approved."

Now Dan stepped forward. "We've come a really long way to see it," he said. *Also not a lie . . . yesterday we were in Africa, for heaven's sake.*

Jake's turn. "We didn't know about asking in advance—can we talk to someone else about it?"

The guard looked them over. Amy did her best to appear earnest, eager, and innocent. She made sure not to look at the others, afraid she might break out of character if she did.

The guard reached for the phone in front of him. "I'll make a call," he said. "But I'm warning you, you probably won't be allowed to see it. This might take a while, so"—he nodded toward a clear acrylic display stand on the desk—"in the meantime I suggest you look around. There's some interesting stuff upstairs."

It was just as well, Atticus thought as they climbed the wide staircase to the mezzanine. *This will give us a chance to check out the building. Plus, it reinforces our cover story.*

The Beinecke was really a building inside a building: In the center was a multistory glass tower. On every floor of the tower were shelves full of books visible through the glass walls.

Old books.

Really old books.

"Incunabula," Atticus said, his eyes glowing with excitement.

"In what?" Dan asked.

"Incunabula," Atticus repeated. "It actually means 'in the cradle.' It's the word used to describe the earliest books ever made."

He tilted his head back to look at the top of the tower, then gazed at the marble walls, turning slowly in a full circle. Now that they were inside, he could see that the white marble slabs were veined with translucent streaks.

"It's so smart!" he said. "See how the marble has those streaks in it? Only a little light can get through—direct light is really bad for old books, it fades them. They're protected from the sun, but you can see them through the glass."

Amy was right there with him. "And they're so beautiful," she said.

Row upon row of books, most of them bound in leather, reached to the ceiling several stories over their heads, illuminated by the faint glow of autumn sunlight through the marble. It was truly striking.

Amy and Atticus paired up for a gushing session as they walked around the mezzanine.

"The brochure says this exhibit is about how a book gets made. That could be interesting. It's *D'Aulaires' Greek Myths* — "

"I LOVE that book! Look, they've got the original drafts — "

"And the preliminary sketches for the artwork! It's showing every step of how the book was made — how cool is that?"

"Not *that* cool," Dan muttered. He and Jake trailed behind, keeping the book-geekery at a safe distance.

Amy gasped. "Atticus, do you see what I see?" She pointed at a display case in one corner of the mezzanine.

In the dim light, Atticus could not make out any details, but he could see that the book in the case was positively enormous.

"Audubon?" he whispered, barely daring to hope.

"It's gotta be," she said, and they raced over.

It was indeed John James Audubon's *Birds of America*, first published in the 1840s. The gigantic book was open to the page for the chickadee, although the caption called it the "Black-Capt Titmouse."

"The original double-elephant folio edition," Atticus said reverently.

"I never thought I'd see one in real life!" Amy said. "Look at the detail—it's absolutely exquisite!"

"I don't see any elephants," Dan complained, "just birds."

Atticus looked at him with pity. "It's the size," he explained. "Elephant folio is big, and after that is 'atlas'—you've probably seen some huge atlases—and then double-elephant, which is the biggest there is."

He furrowed his brow. "I can't think of another book this size, can you?" he asked Amy, who shook her head.

"Whales are bigger than elephants," Jake said. "Why didn't they call it the blue-whale folio?"

"Good one," Dan said and held out his fist toward Jake, who bumped it obligingly.

Amy rolled her eyes at Atticus. "Just ignore them," she said.

It was a wise strategy, because their geekery reached even greater heights at the next case.

"Oh. My. God." Amy put one hand over her heart and clutched Atticus's arm with the other.

"A Gutenberg Bible," Atticus said, and clutched her back for all he was worth.

On the other side of the case, Dan and Jake shook their heads at the same time.

"I'll bite," Dan said with a sigh. "I've heard of it, but what's so special about it?"

"There's something like forty-seven or forty-eight copies left in the whole world," Atticus said. "This book right here? It's worth *millions*."

"Wow, really?" Jake said. "Okay, I'm impressed."

"The Chinese were the first in the world to produce books using movable type and printing presses," Amy said, "but the Gutenberg Bible was the first book made that way in the Western world."

"And then the demand for glasses—I mean, eyeglasses, not drinking glasses"—the words tumbled out of Atticus, he was so excited—"it exploded! Before, books had to be written out by hand, so they were really expensive, so hardly anyone could afford them. After the printing press, there were tons more books around, so a lot more people wanted to read them, and it made them realize that they couldn't see clearly and that they needed glasses!"

Amy seemed entranced, and even Dan and Jake were smiling. Atticus beamed back at them. Not for the first time, he felt grateful for his friendship with Dan, and now Amy. *They know I'm a total nerd, but they actually* like *that about me.*

It reminded him of the way his mother used to treat him. A nice change from being seen as a freak.

He walked slowly around the case with Amy, examining and admiring the book from all sides.

But Dan had moved toward the railing of the mezzanine and was staring at the glass tower.

"Hey," he called softly to the others. "The Voynich—do you think it's somewhere in there?"

CHAPTER 8

Dan's question abruptly altered the mood. Jake, Atticus, and Amy joined him by the railing.

"That's the first thing, isn't it?" Amy said. "Find out where it is."

"Actually, we might not need to," Dan said. "If they bring it out for us, we can snatch it then."

"Yeah, that would be ideal," she said. "But I still think we need to find out where they store it, just in case."

They descended the stairs and stopped at the desk again. The guard recognized them.

"Hold on a second," he said, and lifted the phone. "Dr. James? Those kids I was telling you about, they're here now."

A few moments later, a woman stepped out from a door behind the desk. She was slender and pale, with dark eyes and chin-length auburn hair. The name badge on a lanyard around her neck read: KATHRYN JAMES, CURATOR FOR EARLY MODERN BOOKS & MANUSCRIPTS.

"Hello," she said. "I'm Kathryn James."

Amy went into her act again: homeschoolers on a field trip, studying the medieval period in general and the Voynich in particular. This time Jake and Dan chipped in.

"I've been interested in the Voynich for years," Jake said. "I can't believe I'm finally in the same building with it!"

Dr. James smiled. "I'm afraid we can't show it to you," she said. "As I'm sure you know, the manuscript is very fragile. We have to keep it under restricted access to preserve it."

The four teens exchanged glances of disappointment.

Dr. James went on, "I'm sorry about that, but I can take you downstairs to the reading room, and you can have a look at the catalog. We have lots of Voynich resources that might interest you."

"That would be great," Amy said politely.

Jake guessed what she was thinking: that any chance to see more of the building could be useful. They followed Dr. James around a corner, where she asked them to leave their bags and backpacks in the lockers that lined the wall. Then they went down some stairs and past another guard into the reading area.

They stopped at the desk and signed in. Dr. James then led them to the computers and sat down in front of one. A few clicks later, she had pulled up a page listing the Voynich-related material held by the Beinecke.

Jake ran his eyes down the list, then gasped. "The Marci Letter is kept here, too? Cool!" He turned to the others. "It's from the seventeenth century," he said, "supposedly the earliest surviving written evidence of the manuscript's history."

Dr. James looked surprised first, then impressed. "You do know your Voynich," she said.

"Mostly because of my mom," Jake said. Struck by sudden inspiration, he said, "Maybe you knew her—Astrid Rosenbloom?"

Now Dr. James looked *really* surprised. "Astrid? She's your mom?"

"Yes, did you ever meet her?" Atticus asked eagerly.

Somewhat belatedly, Jake said, "I'm Jake Rosenbloom, and this is my brother, Atticus."

"I should have guessed—you look like her." Dr. James smiled at Atticus. Then she grew solemn and her voice dropped a little. "I was so sorry to hear about her passing."

An uncomfortable silence.

Jake wondered how long it took before you could talk about someone who had died with comfortable silences.

"And yes, I did meet her. We e-mailed each other a lot, and she came here once to view the manuscript."

"She did? When?" Jake asked, a little indignant that Astrid hadn't invited him to go along.

"Summer," Dr. James said. "Not this past one, of course—the summer before. In June, maybe?"

That would have been just before she got sick, Jake thought. *Probably while I was away.* He had spent that summer working as a junior counselor at an eco-camp.

"She came here with . . ." Dr. James paused and gave Jake a quick look he couldn't interpret. "Do you know Dr. Siffright?" she asked.

Jake shook his head. "I don't think so."

"Oh. Well." For the first time, Dr. James seemed to fumble for the right words. "They viewed the manuscript together. Dr. Siffright is — um, very intense about the Voynich."

"You mean she's one of the angels-and-aliens crowd?" Jake asked in surprise. He knew that Astrid had always found those theories ludicrous.

"Oh, no, nothing like that!" Dr. James said hastily. "Dr. Siffright is a reputable scholar! But most academics have several subjects that interest them. Dr. Siffright is — how should I put it — very single-minded."

"I get it," Jake said. Since both his parents were academics, he knew the kind of people Dr. James was talking about. A little batty, but often entertaining when they weren't boring you to death.

"Anyway, I'm glad I got to meet Astrid," Dr. James said. "I enjoyed our exchanges — we had some great discussions."

She looked from Jake to Atticus and back again. Then she clicked through to the home screen on the computer and stood up.

"I'm going to make an exception to the rules," she said, "in memory of Astrid. Let's go to my office."

Dr. James led them through a corridor behind the reading room. At the back of the group, Dan gave Atticus a subtle thumbs-up. So far, the plan—if you could call it that—was working.

In her office, Dr. James made a quick call and a young man named Michael came into her office. She introduced him to the group, then sent him to fetch the Voynich Manuscript.

A few minutes later, Michael wheeled a cart into the office. Dr. James took the manuscript out of its storage box and placed it on a foam wedge to support it.

Jake gasped. "It's so small!" he said. "I thought it would be way bigger!"

The Voynich Manuscript was about the size of an average paperback book, thick, but not large. It looked like a book, too, its pages bound between flimsy leather covers.

"That's a common reaction," Dr. James said. "I think it's because people who view the manuscript are used to studying the digital images. Those were enlarged to show the detail."

Jake reached out with his hand, then stopped and looked anxiously at Dr. James.

"Go ahead," she said. She stepped back and let the rest of them crowd around.

"I can't believe it," Jake murmured, clearly awestruck. "I'm actually *touching* the Voynich!"

He opened the cover gingerly.

"Look at the writing," Amy said. "It's so tiny!"

The pages contained line after line of text in perfect, delicate calligraphy. "That must have taken *forever* to do," Atticus said.

Botanical drawings, astronomical charts, more tiny writing. As Jake paged slowly through the manuscript, occasionally sharing comments with Amy and Atticus, Dan started to feel edgy. *Am I the only one who remembers why we're here?*

"The numbers," he said to Jake. "See the page numbers?"

Each right-hand page had a number in the corner. Ordinary numbers, not in code.

"Those were added long after the manuscript itself was written," Dr. James said, "some think in the seventeenth century. And they're not page numbers, they're folio numbers."

"Duh!" Atticus said and smacked himself on the side of the head in disgust. "I knew that! With old manuscripts, you almost always talk about folios rather than pages. I can't believe I forgot."

"What's a folio?" Dan asked.

"A leaf," Atticus said. He moved closer and held a sheet of the Voynich to demonstrate; it had the number twenty on one side. "One folio equals two pages, see? The first is the recto—that means 'right' in Latin, the right-hand page—"

"Recto?" Dan snickered. "Any relation to the word *rectum*?"

"Actually, yes." It was Dr. James who answered. "The Latin root for both words means 'right,' but it can also mean 'straight.' The rectum is straight, as distinct from the other parts of the intestine."

"Oh," Dan said, blushing.

"Cool!" Atticus said. "Anyway, the other side is the verso, the left-hand page, see?"

Dan put his mind back on task. "Seventy-four," he hissed. "Look up seventy-four."

Jake flipped gingerly through the manuscript. Dan counted under his breath: "Seventy-two, seventy-three, seventy—"

"Hey, look—a plumbing picture!" Atticus said gleefully.

Pools and basins and canals, all filled with naked women. But this time, Dan wasn't interested.

"Turn back one," he said to Jake.

Seventy-three.

"Now forward." To the plumbing picture again.

Amy frowned and leaned closer. "Seventy-five?" she said, and her eyes met Dan's.

About time she caught on!

There was no doubt about it.

Folio 74 was missing.

CHAPTER 9

Dan's thoughts were crashing into one another like a multicar pileup on the highway.

Where is it? Who stole it? It couldn't have been the Vespers — they sent us *to steal it for them! How can we steal it if it isn't here? And if we don't — can't — what will happen to the hostages?*

He saw the stricken expression on Amy's face and knew that she was having the same thoughts.

Dan forced himself to concentrate. *One thing at a time.*

"Do you see that?" He put on a fake-excited voice. "Page seventy-four — it's missing!" Dan turned to Dr. James. "Did you know that already? Or did we, like, discover it?"

Beside him, he could feel Amy's muscles tense.

"We did know about it, but thank you anyway," Dr. James said. "There are several folios missing — the online records give a complete list."

"Do you know when the missing folios disappeared?" Amy asked.

Dr. James shook her head. "No, but they were

already missing when Wilfrid Voynich bought the manuscript."

"In 1912," Jake reminded them.

It seemed that Atticus had finally noticed the Cahills' distress and was puzzling things out, too. "Dr. James, did you just say that the list of missing folios is online?"

"Yes, that's right."

"Oh," Atticus said. "That's nice. That way, ANYONE CAN TELL WHICH ONES ARE MISSING."

In Dan's opinion, Atticus would be well advised to stay away from acting as a career. But his message came through clearly: The Vespers had to know already that Folio 74 was no longer part of the manuscript.

Then why do they still want us to steal it?

Unanswerable, at least for the moment.

The hastily scraped-together plan called for Dan to create a distraction, aided by Amy and Jake. It was Atticus's job to pilfer the manuscript and get it out of the building somehow, the thinking being that as the youngest, he would look the most innocent.

Dan moved away from the manuscript and toward Dr. James. Then he clapped one hand to his eye.

"Ow!" he said. "My contact, I lost my contact!"

He dropped to his knees right next to Dr. James. Just as he hoped, she bent over and began helping him search for the imaginary contact lens.

Then Amy grabbed his elbow.

"It's okay, Dan," she said with a forced smile.

"You—um, you DON'T REALLY NEED IT, do you?"

"What?" Dan almost yelped. *What's with her?! She can't have forgotten the plan already!*

"He doesn't need his contact lens?" Dr. James looked up in surprise.

"Of course I need it!" Dan pulled his arm away from Amy and glared at her. "Thanks for your help, Dr. James. ISN'T SHE NICE TO BE HELPING?"

Amy glared right back at him. "What I meant was, you have all those extra pairs in your suitcase, so THERE'S NO NEED FOR DR. JAMES TO LOOK FOR IT."

Meanwhile, Atticus was edging closer to the manuscript and had one hand on it. Amy reached over and brushed his hand away.

"Atticus, whatever you're thinking about doing, you can't do it now. We need to get going because—because IT'S TIME FOR YOUR NAP."

"My *nap*?" Atticus looked utterly bewildered.

Just then Jake started to say something. "Oh, I get it—er, I mean, you're right, Amy. YOU NEED TO TAKE A NAP, ATTICUS."

Dan still had one hand over his eye. "Will someone please help me find my contact?"

Amy grabbed Atticus with one hand and yanked Dan up with the other. "We should go now," she said, her voice so bright it was almost shrill. "That way we can get Dan another contact and Atticus can have his nap! Thank you, Dr. James, we really appreciate your bending the rules for us."

"You're welcome," Dr. James said, still pleasant but clearly bewildered.

"Yes, thanks, this was great," Jake said. "Really, thank you so much." He put his hand on Dan's shoulder. It might have looked like a friendly gesture, but Jake had a pincer grip and pushed Dan toward the door.

Meanwhile, Amy dragged Atticus out of the room. Without the manuscript.

"A NAP?!" Atticus yelled. "What do you think I am, a three-year-old?"

They were outside the Beinecke once again, after having left the reading area and retrieved their backpacks. On the way out, they had passed two guard stations, as well as the one at the building's entrance.

"Shh," Amy said and led them to a bench.

"What was all that in there, anyway?" Dan said angrily.

"I couldn't very well yell 'Abort, abort!' with Dr. James standing there, could I?" Amy said. "I had to figure out a way to tell you *not* to steal the manuscript."

"I guessed that's what you were doing," Jake said. "And anyway, there were all those guards and they were inspecting everyone's coats and bags. We'd never have gotten away with it."

"But a NAP?" Atticus was still outraged. "Couldn't you have thought of something else?"

"Sorry," Amy said. "I just said the first thing that came to me."

"Why did you call it off?" Dan said. "There might have been something in the manuscript that would tell us where seventy-four is!"

Amy shook her head. "Look. Dr. James and the Beinecke people—they've had the manuscript for years. They've examined it every which way possible. If there was anything in it that pointed to the missing pages, don't you think they'd have figured it out?"

"So why would the Vespers send us here?" Jake asked.

"To see it. So we'd have an idea what we're looking for. I'm not sure, of course, but that's my best bet. The Vespers always know exactly what they want from us, and in this case, it's not the whole manuscript—it's Folio Seventy-four."

Dan refused to be swayed. "I still think—"

"Jake? Atticus? Is that you?"

All four heads turned in the direction of the voice. Across the plaza, they saw someone approaching them.

Atticus couldn't see the man clearly yet. Beside him, Jake rose to his feet.

"Hey, guys!" The man's face broke into a grin and he trotted the last few yards.

"Dave!" Atticus let out a huge sigh of relief.

"He was one of my mom's research assistants,"

Jake explained. "Dave, this is Amy and Dan."

They exchanged greetings, then Dave noogied Atticus's hair. "How are ya, kid?"

"I'm good," Atticus said. "What are you doing here?"

"Working," Dave said. "In the classics department." Then his face grew solemn. "I know I've said it before, but I'm really sorry, guys. Your mom was a great lady. I miss her."

I do, too, Atticus thought, but it seemed too obvious to say. Then his mind went back to the day his mother died. Dave had been at the house. Atticus, Jake, and their dad had taken turns sitting by her bed.

Astrid had been delirious for several days before her death. Tossing restlessly, wringing the sheets and her hands, her eyes open but unseeing. It had been so hard to see her that way. . . .

And she had mumbled a lot. Mostly streams of incomprehensible syllables, but occasionally a few words. Atticus had tried desperately to understand, responding to her as if they were having a normal conversation in the hope of breaking through her delirium.

Already his recollection of her mumblings had helped them once, and he had been meaning to search his memory again. Somehow he hadn't gotten around to it, and he knew why: It was too painful.

But seeing Dave brought it all back—the hours that were endless because of seeing her suffer, and at the same time, much too short because they were her last.

Her words may have been mostly nonsense, but they were his final memory of her.

The Mad King . . . something about guardians . . . stay friends with Dan . . .

And there had been more.

Missing . . . voyage . . . where . . . LaCher . . .

Voyage?

Not voyage — Voynich! She was saying 'Voynich'!

Atticus was thinking so hard that he held his breath, as if any activity other than recollection would take away his ability to remember his mother's words.

"You okay, bud?"

Atticus blinked. Dave was staring at him, looking concerned.

But it wasn't just concern. Atticus frowned. There was something else in Dave's expression, something sharper and less kindly than concern . . . or was he imagining things?

I'm just paranoid over this whole Vesper thing.

"I'm fine," he said. "Sorry — I was thinking about Mom."

Dave nodded. "So, what are you up to? Is your dad here, too?"

"No," Jake said. "We're, um, just here with our friends."

"Dave," Atticus said suddenly, "do you know a friend of Mom's named LaCher?"

"Sure," Dave said. "LaCher Siffright."

Siffright — again?

"Siffright?" Dan said. "That's—" He stopped for a moment, then went on, "That's a funny name."

"She's a medievalist—at Brown, I think," Dave said. "Tall, blond hair . . . Why do you ask?"

"No reason," Atticus said, aware of how lame that sounded. *Quick—think of something else!* "I mean, I was just trying to remember all Mom's friends. I thought maybe—maybe I'd write and ask if they have any pictures of her."

There, that's better. Pretty convincing, if I say so myself. Besides, it's a good idea—I should do it for real.

"Want me to track her down for you?" Dave asked.

"That's okay," Jake said. "I'm sure Dad has her address somewhere."

Dave took out his phone. "Sorry, just thought of something." He took a polite step back, punched in a quick text message, then put the phone away.

"Can I buy you all lunch?" He smiled at Atticus. "Do you still like peanut butter on your tuna-fish sandwich?"

Amy looked at her watch. "That's nice of you, but I'm afraid we need to get going," she said.

Dave glanced at Amy's wrist. "Cool watch," he said. "Okay, I'll get back to work, then. Say hi to your dad for me. And take care, both of you."

Atticus waited until Dave was out of sight. Then he turned to the group and said, "I know what we need to do next."

CHAPTER 10

Ted could sense the heaviness of the depression in the room. He and the other hostages had staked everything on the escape attempt. Now that they had been recaptured, they had nothing left.

It was quiet, with only the occasional sounds of Nellie and Natalie moving about as they attended to Alistair. Nellie should have been a patient herself: During the escape attempt, she had been attacked by the Vespers' dogs.

But Alistair was worse off. He had lost a lot of blood from the deep gash in his leg, which had been cut on a sharp rock as he was trying — unsuccessfully — to keep Phoenix from going over the edge of a cliff.

The wound had gone septic. Alistair had a high fever, and the girls were using up some of their precious water ration to soak rags and place them on his body in an effort to get his temperature down.

Ted could have told them it was no use. The combination of Alistair's advanced years and his weakened constitution left him defenseless. Ted could already smell it — the putrid odor of the infection snaking inexorably through Alistair's system.

Then he heard an odd noise like rapid drumming, followed by Nellie's panicked voice.

"Quick! Turn him on his side!"

Natalie's voice: "Oh, my God, what's happening?"

"He's having a seizure —"

The noise was Alistair's feet beating uncontrollably against the floor. The drumming sound slowed, then stopped as the seizure ended.

"Alistair? Alistair, it's Nellie. Can you hear me?"

Ted heard the slow, strained gasp of Alistair's lungs pulling desperately for air.

"Brave," Alistair croaked. "Amy . . . Dan . . . all of you."

"Alistair!" The anguish in Nellie's voice made Ted flinch.

"Help him!" Natalie's scream bounced off the walls. "Somebody, please! Hurry!"

Ted heard another long, terrible breath that made his scalp tingle and the rest of his body shudder. To him, the sound was as bad as what everyone else was seeing.

Maybe worse.

The silence that followed was absolute.

"Here's what I'm thinking," Atticus said. "We need to —"

Amy's phone sounded with the tone she had programmed for Vesper One's calls. It was a text alerting them to an incoming video transmission. Quickly, Dan got out his laptop so they could see the video on a full screen.

The transmission came through as a Skype call. On the screen they saw Nellie, live, her eyes filled with fury even as tears spilled out of them.

"Amy and Dan? Bad news here. Really bad." Pause. Sniffle.

Amy held her breath.

Nellie looked pale and haggard. She cut her eyes to one side, glancing at something or someone else. After a few moments, she looked straight on again. It seemed to Amy that she was receiving silent cues about what she could and couldn't say on camera.

"He was already so weak, and then he got a cut on his leg. It got infected. And the infection spread really fast. There was nothing we could do. . . ."

Her voice caught; she cleared her throat. "He was thinking of you at the end. He said, 'Brave, Amy and Dan and all of you.' And then—"

Nellie lowered her head and sobbed, unable to speak for a few moments. Then she wiped her eyes and looked into the camera.

"He's gone, kiddos. Uncle Alistair's gone."

For a moment, Amy's vision was blotted out by the black anger that engulfed her whole being. Grief would come later, she knew; for now, she could only feel rage.

"I KNOW YOU CAN HEAR ME!" she screamed at the

computer. "I thought you at least had SOME sense of honor — in your sick, twisted way! HOW COULD YOU DO THIS?"

The image of Nellie's face blipped out and was replaced by the program's placeholder icon. Vesper One's words were creepily robotic, filtered through an electronic voice distorter.

"You have forty-eight hours left." The call disconnected. Dan cursed — not loud, but fiercely. Amy put a hand on his shoulder and felt him trembling with grief and rage.

Amy put her other hand to her neck and deliberately scraped the small powder burn with her fingernail. For some stupid reason she wanted to feel physical pain . . . to match the anguish in her heart.

It hurt. A lot.

"Atticus," Jake said quietly. "Let's go to the car."

Amy gave Jake a look of gratitude, but he had already turned away.

Dan was leaning forward as he sat on the bench, head down, elbows on his knees, picking aimlessly at a loose thread in his jeans. He spoke without looking at her. "Nellie said that he said our names at the end. And 'brave.' Do you think he meant 'Be brave,' or that he thinks we *are* brave?" He didn't wait for her to answer. "Both, I bet. Pretty cool of him."

Yes. Yes, but —

Amy closed her eyes against the heat of her tears.

"Dan," she whispered, "I don't think I can do this anymore."

Dan was silent for a few moments. "I know," he said at last. "It's — it's awful. But, Amy —"

She could feel him shifting his weight, leaning toward her, so she opened her eyes and looked at him.

"Two things. First, it's not like we have a choice," he said. "I mean, what are you gonna do — just give up and abandon the hostages? And second, remember what you told Ham, about how Erasmus and Phoenix would have wanted us to keep going? It's not just something you said to make Jonah feel better. It's the truth."

"But I feel like — like I've got nothing left," she said, "and even that nothing is all beat up and kicked around and trampled on. . . ."

Her voice trailed off. They sat there for what seemed like a long time, their silence a bubble of sadness surrounding them.

Finally, Dan straightened up a little. "I know what we need," he said. "Microwave burritos."

Amy smiled weakly at the mention of Alistair's most famous invention.

"Remember that party he gave at the house?" Dan went on. "Mini-burritos for appetizers, burritos for the main course, and ice-cream burritos for dessert!"

"We took the leftovers to the soup kitchen — how many was it?"

"Eighty-seven," Dan said. "I counted. Alistair was bummed that there were so many left, but man, we were all stuffed—we'd eaten as much as we could!"

"He was a funny duck, for sure," Amy said. "And it took him forever to make up his mind about us. Even though I think he liked us right from the beginning."

"Except for that time he nearly got us blown up." Dan barked out a laugh. "It was almost worth it, to see the look on his face when he saw us again!"

"He was with us during some tough times," Amy said. "Really, he ended up helping us a lot more than—than he hurt us. And after the hunt was over . . ." The rest of her thought stayed clogged in her throat. *He was like an uncle to us. And that's how we thought of him. Uncle Alistair.*

Amy couldn't hold back the tears any longer.

Dan hesitated for only a moment. Then he put an arm around her shoulders as her body shuddered with sobs that only he could hear.

CHAPTER 11

It was a source of satisfaction to Jake that Sinead had left the keys in the SUV's ignition. He had taken them, so now they had a car and she didn't.

It was only a small thing, but it was worth a gloat.

Jake and Atticus sat in the front, Jake in the driver's seat. They were quiet, both thinking about the Cahills and their Uncle Alistair. Jake tried to think of what he could say to Amy to make her feel better.

But that's dumb. When Mom died, I didn't want to feel better—not at first. It really bugged me when everyone kept trying to cheer me up. People need *to feel bad for a while.*

He wished they could take a walk, just him and Amy. *Not gonna happen anytime soon, not with all this craziness.*

And it struck him that this was the way to help her: to figure out the next step.

"Weren't you saying"—Jake tapped Atticus's knee—"that you had an idea about what to do next?"

Atticus perked up. "Yeah, listen. I remembered something else Mom said when she was sick. I thought she was saying *voyage*, but now I know it was *Voynich*. And at the same time she was saying *LaCher*—"

"Siffright," Jake broke in. "That's twice her name has come up."

"So she and Mom were studying the Voynich together," Atticus said. "And I thought—hang on."

He dug into his backpack and took out his laptop. Atticus's laptop had belonged to Astrid; he had taken it for his own after she died. All her files were still on it; he had never erased anything of hers. Jake remembered the early days following her funeral, sitting with Atticus and looking at the computer—reading things she'd written, listening to her playlists, looking at photos.

Which were mostly of himself and Atticus. Almost none of her, as she had always been the one wielding the camera.

"Look," Atticus said. He clicked the Gmail icon. "Dr. James said she and Mom e-mailed each other. Maybe Mom e-mailed Dr. Siffright, too." He sat with his fingers poised over the keyboard. "Username?"

"I know that!" Jake said. "She used it for almost all her stuff. Her first initial and last name—"

"Okay, so 'arosenbloom'—"

"—except she made it a pun, like this: 'a-r-o-s-e-**I**-n-b-l-o-o-m.' Get it? 'A rose in bloom.'" Jake grinned. "Hey, that could be your username, too."

Atticus made a face. "Yeah, right."

He typed in the username. "What about a password?" he asked.

Jake groaned. "Don't have a clue. It could be anything. Try her birthday."

No good. They tried other dates: their dad's birthday and their own, and Atticus even managed to remember the date of their parents' wedding anniversary. Address, zip code, phone number.

More no good.

"Classics stuff, maybe?" Atticus suggested. He tried several famous Greek and Latin names and titles of works that Astrid had loved. "Homer" and *"Iliad"* didn't work. Neither did "Plutarch," "Sophocles," or "Herodotus," "Electra," "Orpheus," and every Greek god they could think of. All epic fails.

"Any one of those could be right, but if she added numbers to the end, we're screwed," Jake said.

Atticus frowned. "Mom wasn't a numbers person. She always said names were easier for her to remember than dates."

Jake sat up straighter. "In that case—" He reached over and turned the laptop toward him so he could type on it. Eleven dots filled the password space. He hit RETURN.

Bingo—her inbox!

"Cool!" Atticus exclaimed. "What was it?"

"Your idea," Jake said. "You said names, so I typed in ours."

Astrid's password was JAKEATTICUS.

The brothers smiled at each other, more happy than sad.

"Dan! Amy! Come quick—we found something!"

Atticus was hanging halfway out of the car window, waving wildly.

Amy and Dan broke into a run.

Amy hadn't thought it possible for her to feel any more urgency about the hostages than she already felt. But Alistair's death had doubled her dread.

They got into the backseat and Atticus shoved the laptop at them.

"Do these numbers mean anything to you?"

It was a long list of numbers separated by colons:

1:2	26:3	40:5
5:1	4:2	44:5
10:3	25:2	38:1
12:3	33:3	5:2
12:6	9:1	40:2
20:2	36:1	46:1
		27:1

Amy shook her head. Dan shrugged. "What are they?" he asked.

"We don't know, either," Atticus said.

"Wait," Jake said. "We need to back up a little." He explained about getting into Astrid's e-mail account. "And we found some e-mails from LaCher Siffright. She sent them right before Mom died. Look."

Jake toggled to the inbox and clicked on one of the messages.

```
Time for me to go on vacation! How are
you? I realized that I need a break, so
I'm hunkering down at one of my favorite
spots. I'll send you some more info about
this lovely site. Promise me you'll take
care of yourself!
Cheers, LaCher
```

"And then she sent this one, with the numbers, on the same day."

```
Astrid: Here are the figures you
requested. Hope these work for you.
Cheers, LaCher
```

```
P.S. Don't forget the lucky horsemen!
```

"Lucky horsemen? What's that about?" Amy asked. It was almost as if she had spoken automatically. Or as if only a part of her had asked the question. The other part was still with the hostages . . . and Uncle Alistair.

On the one hand, it felt wrong to be torn so quickly from thinking about him; on the other, she was grateful to have something that took her thoughts away from his death.

Always complicated. Will things ever be simple again?

"No clue," Jake answered. "Mom didn't have anything to do with horses or racing or anything like that."

"Anyway, I typed all the numbers into a document," Atticus said. "We thought it might help us figure out what they are. But so far, no luck."

"Bible verses?" Dan said.

"That's what I thought, too," Atticus said. "But without the names of the books?"

"They look like ratios," Jake said.

"What about longitude and latitude?" Amy wondered.

Dan shook his head. "That's usually commas, not colons," he said. "I'm sure both Dr. Siffright and your mom knew that."

Amy frowned, thinking hard. "Read them aloud," she said.

"The whole list?" Atticus asked.

"Not the numbers. The e-mails."

"I'll do it," Jake said. He read the first one, slowly and clearly.

Amy closed her eyes in concentration. Jake finished reading; she opened her eyes to see him staring at her. She felt a tiny thrill and blinked rapidly to banish it.

"I get it," he said. "It's weird, right? Is that what you're thinking?"

Well, not exactly. But she nodded and furrowed her brow, bringing her mind back on task. "The 'How are you?' seems out of place, for one thing," she said.

"And why would you write about a vacation without saying where you're going?" Jake pointed out.

"Did you find anything where your mom requested

numbers from her?" Amy asked.

"No, nothing like that," Atticus said. "She was already sick by then—in bed most of the time, and she couldn't do any work. She never replied to either of these. Besides, look at the time stamp." He tapped back and forth between the two messages. "Dr. Siffright sent the second one right after the first."

"What about e-mails before those ones?" Dan asked.

"There's a few from when they went to see the Voynich," Atticus said. "Just normal stuff, like what time they should meet. And one more—after Yale, Dr. Siffright went to Italy and wrote that she was poking around in old monasteries there. And that's all. If there was anything else from her, Mom didn't save it."

"Okay," Dan said and took a breath. "I'm guessing that the two e-mails are, like, related. In some kind of code."

"Yeah, I could see that," Atticus said. "So what have we got? The first number in each pair is almost always bigger. But the second number—"

"All single digits," Dan said. "And random. Or at least, they look random."

Atticus dragged the two e-mails so they were side by side on the screen. He passed the laptop around, and each of them studied the screen in turn.

"I think we should concentrate on the first e-mail," Amy said. "There's more to work with. We have to figure out why it's so weird—why she wrote it the way she did."

Jake stared at her, but this time, she could tell that he wasn't seeing her. He took the laptop and his gaze flicked between the two e-mails.

"What is it?" she asked.

"I was wondering . . . what Dan said. If the numbers have some kind of relationship to the words."

"That's it!" Atticus almost shouted. "The numbers go with the e-mail!"

"How?" All three of the others spoke at once.

Atticus laced his fingers together and stretched out his arms, cracking his knuckles. "Prepare to be amazed, people," he said. "Paper and pencil, please? Or, Dan, your laptop."

Looking at the two e-mails, Atticus called out letters that Dan typed into a new document.

"I get it now!" Dan exclaimed. "The first number is the word, and the second number is the letter!"

"Elementary, my dear Cahill," Atticus said gleefully.

1:2. First word, second letter. I.

5:1: Fifth word, first letter. G.

When they finished, Dan had a string of letters on his screen:

I G U A Z U V O Y F A L L S P O O L S

And a few clicks later, Atticus looked up from *his* screen. "Anyone speak Portuguese?" he said. "Next stop, Brazil!"

CHAPTER 12

The text message had been brief in the extreme:

AS DISCUSSED.

It meant that the plan was a go.

Vesper Two peered out of the hotel room window. The hotel itself was acceptable. The city in which it was located was not. Of course, very few cities met Vesper Two's standards for luxury, convenience, and culture. London, of course. Paris, if it weren't for all those French people. New York, ditto Americans.

This city was none of the above, and Vesper Two could hardly wait to leave it.

A most excellent plan. *V-1 should have credited my genius for more. As if calling me his little scorpion is enough.*

Vesper Two's jaw clenched, and it took a few deep breaths before calm returned.

Yes . . . calm. A cool head.

Just another couple of days, and I'll be able to make my move. Once this task is accomplished, the rest of the Vespers will all fall in behind me. Take care of the Cahills, and V-1 will go down with them.

And the new V-1? That would be moi, *of course.*

Vesper Two opened a suitcase and began packing.

Iguazu. Iguaçu. Iguassu.

The name was spelled several different ways, but all the Internet sources agreed on one thing: Iguazu had spectacular waterfalls. *Foz do Iguazu,* the falls of Iguazu.

IGUAZU. VOY. FALLS. POOLS.

It was a long trip: First the drive back to New York, then a flight to São Paulo, and finally a puddle-jumper from São Paulo to Foz do Iguazu.

On the last flight, Amy sat next to Jake, with Dan and Atticus a few rows ahead of them. As they took their seats, Amy reminded herself firmly to keep her mind on the mission—not on the fact that Jake was sitting only inches away from her.

Jake started talking about Dr. Siffright's message. "The P.S. to the second e-mail—we still haven't figured that out," he said. "'Lucky horsemen.' It has to mean something. Champion jockeys?"

"Fortunate ranchers," Amy responded, relieved to have something to focus on.

"Cowboys who win the lottery?"

They smiled at each other, but only briefly.

"Okay, so let's try another approach," Amy

suggested. "Break it down. Start with 'lucky.' Four-leaf clovers."

"Rabbit's foot."

"Horseshoe."

"The number seven—" Jake's eyes widened.

"Seven," she echoed. "So we would need a four—"

He was right there with her. "To make seven-four, seventy-four."

"Horsemen . . . and the number four—"

It hit them both at the same time.

"The Four Horsemen of the Apocalypse!" they said together.

Amy held up her hand for a high five. Jake slapped it, then turned the slap into an awkward handshake that lasted a whole lot longer than normal.

Is he trying to hold my hand?

Amy's heart sped up a little as she pulled her hand away and pretended to fiddle with her seat belt.

Disembarking, Jake and Amy told the younger boys about their discovery.

"Wow," Atticus said. "That confirms it. She was really smart about it. Even if you decoded the message, it still only says 'VOY,' not Voynich. And then she made the clue about Folio Seventy-four separate. So someone would have to know exactly what she was talking about to figure out the whole thing."

For the first time since Alistair's death, Amy's spirits

lifted a little.

Brave — Dan was right. He was proud of us for being brave, but he was also telling us to keep being brave. I'll try, Uncle Alistair, I really will. . . .

The Iguazu airport was a small one. The arrivals hall was lined with booths offering tourist services — hotels, taxis, tours. At a currency exchange booth, Amy changed dollars into Brazilian *reais*; the clerk told her it was pronounced something like "hey-ice."

That'll take some practice, she thought, and repeated the word a couple of times. The word for the local currency was an important one to know.

They headed outside to catch a taxi. About a dozen people were standing in line.

To the right of the line was an empty stretch of pavement. Two young men and a woman emerged from the arrivals hall; they were dressed all in white, loose trousers and T-shirts. Amy recognized the pants as martial-arts gear, similar to what Sensei Takamoto wore for lessons. The two men were shaved bald; the woman had her dark hair in a braid down her back.

One of them set up a boom box on the pavement, and Latin-sounding music with a syncopated drumbeat blared from the speakers. Taking up positions in a triangle, the threesome began an impressive display.

They kicked and twirled in a mock fight, using techniques that seemed drawn from every kind of martial art: kickboxing, tae kwon do, karate. Mixed in were acrobatics and hip-hop-type dance moves.

It was amazing. At one point, one of the men did a handstand and held it for at least a minute, changing the position of his legs, hopping around on his hands, piking so his shoulders almost turned inside out, then straightening again into a perfect vertical.

Meanwhile, the other two went into a series of butterflies — like sideways no-handed cartwheels. The woman would do a butterfly, legs kicking right at her partner's face; the man would duck at the last moment and spin into a butterfly of his own, almost kicking *her* in the face. If either had been a split second off in the timing, there could have been a nasty collision.

The whole taxi line was mesmerized. The man standing next to them nudged Jake. "That's capoeira," he said. "Brazilian martial art. Cool, isn't it?"

Amy made a mental note to add capoeira to the Cahill training regimen. *With moves like that, I could have kicked Sinead's butt!*

The music came to an end. The woman, still panting from exertion, picked up a baseball cap and went down the line. Amy threw in a lavender five-*reais* note, worth around three dollars.

The woman bowed and set the cap down. The three capoeiristas took long drinks from their water bottles. Then the woman walked over to the boom box to start the music again.

Amy was glad; she wanted to see more. Atticus moved over a few steps to get a better view. Another incredible display: flips and floor moves, each step precise but relaxed at the same time, the discipline of Asian martial arts infused with a laid-back Brazilian attitude.

Then there was a little break in the action: The woman gestured to Atticus.

"Who, me?" he said, startled.

She smiled and took him by the arm to the middle of the pavement. The trio began doing their moves in a circle, with Atticus in the center.

"Cool!" he said.

The athletes continued their display. Atticus grinned at the others self-consciously. "Watch," he said. "I'm not gonna flinch, no matter how close they get." He crossed his arms and took on an unblinking expression.

Twirl, flip, spin, kick. The circle seemed to be tightening. *They* are *getting a little close,* Amy thought. Beside her, Jake shifted uncomfortably.

Atticus seemed unfazed, or at least was pretending to be. The music increased in speed, the drumbeats almost frenzied now.

Then the woman whirled and jumped into the air doing a scissors kick. She caught Atticus behind the knees and with a cry of alarm, he went down in a heap.

The capoeiristas stopped abruptly as Amy, Jake, and Dan rushed toward Atticus.

"*Tenho pena*—sorry, sorry!" the woman said and bent over Atticus as he lay sprawled on the pavement.

"Atticus!" Jake dropped to one knee beside his brother.

Atticus gasped and coughed, but at the same time, he held up a finger to let everyone know he was okay.

"Wind knocked out of me," he wheezed.

"You're bleeding, too," Dan pointed out.

Atticus looked at his wrist, which was bleeding from a pavement burn. "Ouch," he said, a little belatedly.

Amy burrowed through her bag for a tissue and hand sanitizer. "Here," she said. "Put some of this on it."

"Sorry, so sorry," the female capoeirista said again. She stopped the music and picked up the boom box at Amy's feet. Suddenly, she turned toward Amy with her eyes narrowed.

"Um, dois, três," she said.

"Pardon?" Amy asked.

The capoeirista looked at her coldly. *"Um, dois, três,"* she repeated. Then she muttered something that sounded like "more" and "a little less" and "a bell," and pushed past Amy to rejoin her companions.

What was that all about? "Um, dois, três" — *that must be "one, two, three" in Portuguese. And the rest didn't make any sense, so it was probably Portuguese, too. But why did she give me that nasty look?*

As they got into a taxi, Amy decided she was imagining things. If it had been a deliberate attack — a far-fetched idea to begin with — it wasn't a very good one: Atticus was nearly unscathed.

Just now he was asking Dan a typical Atticus question: "Do you think they say 'ouch' here in Brazil? Or do you have a whole different word for it?"

CHAPTER 13

Dan had never seen anything like it.

It wasn't just one waterfall, or a central waterfall with a sideshow or two. Iguazu Falls was *hundreds* of waterfalls, spilling over the rim of a huge horseshoe-shaped plateau.

Magical, Dan thought. *That might be the only word for it.*

"Two hundred seventy-four waterfalls," Amy said, reading from the brochure she had picked up at the ticket counter. Among the tourists, camera shutters were clicking so furiously that they sounded like a horde of strange mechanical insects.

Dan put his backpack down on the ground and took out his cell phone so he could take some photos, too.

"Dan!" Atticus tugged on Dan's arm. "Quick, get a photo of THEM!"

Turning away from the rail, Dan saw half a dozen animals approaching. They looked like big raccoons. Except they were mostly tan, instead of gray. And had long snouts instead of bandit masks. Their tails were striped like a raccoon's, but were much longer and thinner. And they weren't the least bit afraid of humans, coming within an arm's length of the group.

Dan began snapping photos from every angle.

"What are they?" Jake asked.

"Coatis," Amy said, reading from the brochure again.

"Co-whattees?" Dan said.

"Coatimundis," Amy said. "It says, 'Please do not feed or touch them.' It also says they're very curious—"

Atticus laughed. "Look at that one!"

A coati was investigating Dan's backpack. It had managed to undo a couple of the Velcro flaps and was busy emptying a compartment. It pulled out a few small plastic vials, then a ziplock bag, and began pawing at them.

The serum ingredients!

"HEY!" Dan shouted and rushed toward the coati.

He grabbed the pack and tried to shoo the coati away. Hastily he picked up the items and put them back into the compartment. Then he searched the ground to make sure nothing else had been pulled out.

"Get out of here, you stupid co-whatever-you-are," he said angrily.

The coati stood up on its hind legs in front of Dan, as if it were begging.

Atticus giggled. "I don't think it understood you. Maybe if you spoke to it in Portuguese—"

"Very funny," Dan said, hoisting the pack a little higher. "I just don't want it messing with my stuff."

"It's only looking for food," Amy said.

"Yeah, Dan, it's not interested in your dirty under-wear," Jake said with a snicker.

Dan didn't dare make eye contact with Amy. *Did she see . . . ?* He aimed an air-kick at the offending coati. "Leave my stuff alone," he muttered.

"Hey, chill," Atticus said. "It's no big deal, right?"

Dan gritted his teeth. "Right," he said. "No big deal."

The path to the river level of the park descended in a series of switchbacks supplemented by an occasional set of stairs, all under the canopy of the Brazilian rain forest. At the bottom of the last set of stairs, they saw a broad walkway flanked by metal railings. It extended several hundred yards out over the Iguazu River and ended in a viewing platform.

They walked toward the platform, Dan and Atticus leading the way. Jake could feel a cool dampness in the air; a few more steps and mist from the waterfalls began coming down on them in earnest. The tourists on their way back from the platform were very wet.

Jake got a peculiar feeling at the back of his neck. He flipped up the collar of his jacket to keep the mist off.

But it's not the wetness. It feels more like . . . like we're being followed.

He took a quick glance over his shoulder.

A crowd of tourists, any one of whom could have been following them. They all looked innocent enough, but what did he expect—someone who looked like a spy?

"What is it?" Amy asked. Somehow she was keyed in to his thoughts; he saw the immediate tension in her shoulders even though her voice was calm.

Don't get her all upset, Jake told himself. *The fun meter crashes when she freaks out. Besides, it's probably nothing.*

He smiled reassuringly. "Just a little game I play when I'm in a tourist place," he said, "seeing if I can guess the nationalities." Which was true—he and Atticus sometimes did this together.

She raised her eyebrows. "So what do you look for?"

"Well, let's see . . ." He nodded toward a couple a few yards ahead of them. "Blond, big backpacks, Birkenstocks. My guess, either German or Dutch."

"What about me?" she asked. "If you didn't know me, would you guess I'm American?"

He put his hand on his chin, pretending to be in deep thought. "I'd have to say . . . Mars. Definitely Martian."

Amy rolled her eyes and shook her head. "Figures. I knew you couldn't be serious about this."

Jake cocked his head and examined her head to toe.

She looked self-conscious now. "What?"

He held up one hand. "Welcome, Martian female. Greetings from Earthling male."

She laughed.

It felt great to make her laugh.

They caught up with Atticus and Dan on the viewing platform, where the mist was so heavy it was like being rained on while standing in the middle of a cloud. None of them minded getting wet with the air so warm.

All four stood silent in wonder at the beauty around them. Green rain forest. Blue sky. Birds floating lazily on the thermal wind currents—a big black hawk flying solo, a flock of primary-colored parrots. The white foam of the falls complete with a double rainbow, sunlight refracted through the spray . . .

Dan was the first to speak, his words blurred by the roar of the cascading water. "Pools," he said. "What about the pools?"

"Poos?" Amy said.

"What poos?" Atticus asked. "Bird poos? It's called guano. Actually, it's pretty interesting how many different words there are for animal poos. *Guano*, *dung*, *droppings*, *spoors*, *cow pies*, *buffalo chips* . . . One of my favorites is *fewmets*."

Dan said, "But I didn't—"

"*Fewmets*—that's from medieval times, the poo you find when an animal is being hunted on a quest." Atticus was on a roll again. "And did you know that otter poo is called spraints?"

"Why do otters get their own word for poo?" Jake wondered.

"I love otters, they're so playful," Amy said. "*Spraints*—what a funny word."

"Enough with the poos!" Dan yelled. Then he looked

at Atticus. "I mean, it's cool—especially about the spraints, I didn't know that before—but I didn't say *poos*."

"You didn't?" Atticus looked puzzled. "Then why are we talking about it?"

Dan threw up his hands. "Forget it—can I start over? I didn't say poos. I said *POOLS*."

"Oh. *Pools*." Atticus's brain made the immediate switch. "You mean, in Dr. Siffright's message?"

"Yeah. Iguazu, Voy, Falls—check, check, and check," Dan said. "But there's no pools. Just the river."

Jake had almost forgotten the reason they were there. He dropped his gaze from the heights of the falls to the river around the platform.

"The water's a little calmer here," he said.

"But you couldn't call it a pool," Atticus pointed out.

"Still, we should have a good look around," Amy said.

Reluctantly, they turned away from the view and began walking back. By unspoken agreement, they split up, Dan and Atticus on one side, Jake and Amy on the other.

Jake kept his head down, inspecting every inch around him. It was hard to believe that Dr. Siffright would have hidden a valuable manuscript folio in such a wet location, but he searched diligently anyway. It was slow going.

Then he got that feeling in his neck again.

CHAPTER 14

Jake straightened up and looked around. Most of the crowd they had arrived with had left by now, replaced by new waves of tourists. Was there anyone familiar — someone he had seen before?

Maybe . . . it could have been the same person. Wait — I'm sure now, I recognize those clothes . . . But there's no law against anyone hanging out here as long as they want. . . .

Then Atticus called out, "Hey, guys?"

The group met in the middle of the walkway. "We're only searching *half* of this place," Atticus said. "There's a whole other half we can't see."

They all looked at him blankly.

Atticus pointed down toward his feet. "Underneath," he said.

Boy Genius strikes again, Jake thought as he hurried with the others to the side.

They peered over the railing. The walkway and platform were supported by concrete pylons sunk deep into the riverbed. The water was at least twenty feet below.

"It'd be easy to climb over," Dan said. "I could hang

on to the railing and maybe get a look—"

"NO," Amy said. "Don't even start."

"He's right," Jake said. Amy glared at him, so he went on hurriedly, "And so are you. All we would need is a harness and some rope. You could do it sort of rock-climbing style and it would be safe."

Amy still looked doubtful. "We'd have to come back after the park is closed and sneak in somehow."

"Shouldn't be too hard," Dan said. "They don't have anything like the security at museums."

Amy nodded. "Okay. But let's finish searching up here. You never know, if we find something we might not have to come back."

Dan and Atticus returned to their side. Jake stood at the railing a little longer, trying to envision the best way to fix a rope so they could examine the supporting structure.

With Amy and the boys covering the sides, Jake decided to move toward the middle of the walkway. Up ahead, a large crowd walked toward him; they were led by a tour guide who held a red umbrella high over her head so the group could keep her in sight easily. On Jake's left was a gaggle of elementary-school kids in their uniforms of white shirts and navy shorts. To his right, several paces behind Dan and Atticus, Jake saw a man with dark hair in a ponytail, carrying a musical instrument—a long straight pipe made of bamboo. The man stopped walking and raised the pipe to his lips.

Jake frowned as his mind began to tick off things

that weren't quite right.

Doesn't make sense — it would be too hard to hear the music with all the noise from the falls.

And that pipe — there aren't any holes in it. So how can it be a musical instrument? It looks more like —

There was a cold, calculating look on the man's face. He closed one eye and squinted along the length of the pipe.

Like he's aiming at something . . .

Aiming? Then it's definitely not a musical instrument. It's some kind of — of blowpipe.

Which meant that it was a weapon.

And it was pointed directly at Atticus.

Slow motion.

Fast action.

An impossible combination, but that was what it felt like to Jake.

Atticus was standing next to Dan, about ten feet away. Jake yelled and ran toward them, covering the distance in two giant strides. Then he launched himself off his feet and knocked his brother into the railing.

Something whistled past his ear.

The brothers both ended up on the ground. Jake threw himself on top of Atticus, who immediately began squirming in protest.

"Stay still!" Jake warned and moved to cover Atticus

with his body.

"Like I have a choice?" Atticus's voice was muffled beneath him. "What the heck is going on?"

Jake raised his head cautiously. "You stay down," he said to Atticus. He stood up and scanned the crowd.

No sign of Mr. Blowpipe. *Whoever he is, he knows what he's doing. Not running away—that would have made him stand out.* The man had simply melted into the crowd.

"Hey, guys?"

A few steps away, Dan was staring at something in his hand.

"My shoulder," he said vaguely. "I'm not sure, but . . ."

Dan's legs buckled beneath him. He dropped whatever he was holding. Jake only just managed to grab one of his arms in time to break his fall.

"Dan!" Atticus scrambled on his knees to get near his friend. "What happened? What's wrong?"

Jake lowered Dan to the ground. Then he searched the area around them frantically and found what he was looking for—the thing Dan had dropped.

A blow dart.

Dan was still conscious, but seemed unable to speak.

"DOCTOR!" Jake shouted. "Help, help! Is anyone here a doctor?"

A woman stepped forward out of the small crowd that was already forming. "Someone call an ambulance," she said. "And can the rest of you give me some space?" She had a brisk Irish accent.

"Here," Jake said. "He got hit with this." Carefully he handed the woman the dart.

"You're joking," she said, but saw immediately that he wasn't. She nodded, tight-lipped, then knelt next to Dan.

Jake's shouts brought Amy running from the other side of the walkway. "What's going on — oh, my God — Dan!" She threw herself down next to him.

"Is it his asthma?" she asked frantically. "But he's been so much better lately — he's never collapsed before — where's his inhaler?" She began scrabbling around, trying to check Dan's pockets.

"It's not asthma. Help me roll him onto his back, please," the doctor said, distracting Amy just before her panic soared out of control.

They got Dan onto his back, then the doctor asked for a jacket. Amy whipped hers off and folded it into a pillow, which was placed under Dan's head.

By now, Dan was clutching at his throat and gasping for breath. The helplessness in his eyes as he looked at her made her want to howl like a wounded animal.

"Take it easy, Dan," she said. To her astonishment, her voice was steady, even as tears began streaming down her face.

This can't be happening. No no no no no . . . Amy reached out her hand without even knowing it, clawing mutely at the air in the direction of the doctor.

"I'm guessing curare," the doctor said, calm and urgent at the same time. She shook her head. "How in the world — never mind." She rolled up her sleeves and took Amy by the shoulders. "Are you his sister? You can stay here, but I need to work on him, all right?"

The doctor began performing CPR on Dan, pumping his chest rhythmically.

Dan looked so frail now, under the doctor's insistent hands. Didn't people's breastbones sometimes break if CPR wasn't done correctly? But she was a doctor; surely she knew what she was doing. *Please please please . . .*

"Can I help?" Amy was sobbing, but still managed to get the words out.

"Just hold his hand," the doctor said. "You can talk to him if you like."

Amy wiped her tears with her sleeve. "Dan? Hang in there, Dan. There's a doctor here helping you —" *What a stupid thing to say, with her leaning right on his chest.*

She couldn't go on, couldn't do anything more than squeeze his hand.

Atticus scooted around until he was next to Amy

and crouched beside her. "Amy?" he said in a low voice. "She said 'curare.' I've read about it; it comes from tropical plants. You put it on a dart and shoot it, and it paralyzes your prey. It stops breathing, that's what kills—"

Amy's mouth opened, closed, opened again.

She needed to scream. And hit something. Or somebody.

But she couldn't move or make a single sound. It was as if she, too, was paralyzed.

"Atticus, stop it!" Jake said angrily.

"I wasn't finished—"

"Shut up! You're not helping!"

"No, YOU shut up!" Atticus retorted fiercely.

The outburst was so un-Atticus-like that Jake and Amy both stared at him, mouths agape. In the silence that followed, they could hear the doctor counting quietly as she continued working on Dan.

Atticus spoke earnestly. "The effects of the poison aren't permanent. If she does CPR on him, keeps his blood pumping and getting oxygen to his brain, it'll wear off, and he should be able to breathe on his own again."

"Atticus, are you sure about this?" Jake asked. "You better be—"

"I'm sure, I swear it! Animals that get hunted, nobody does CPR on them, that's why they die. That's why she's doing CPR now!"

Amy grabbed Atticus's arm, feeling almost torn in two between fear and hope.

"How long?" she gasped out. "How long until he can breathe by himself?"

Then the doctor spoke, in between counts. "One—two—three—four—Depends," she said, "on how much—two—three—four—poison got into him—two—three—four. Where is that ambulance?"

It was a few hours after the attack. Amy sat next to the hospital bed, her face blotchy with tearstains,

He looks younger somehow, she thought. For a moment, Amy felt like she might never be able to move again. But she forced herself to reach for Dan's hand and hold it.

Which he would ordinarily have never let her do in front of the other boys.

Thanks to the good work by the doctor on the scene, as well as the fact that Dan had plucked the dart out almost immediately, he was already breathing on his own. But Amy wouldn't relax until a doctor gave the all-clear sign.

"I'm fine," he declared for about the seventh time. "My arm feels a little weird, that's all."

The nurse put another pillow behind him.

"I should send a—a thank-you note or something," he said. "Did you get her name?"

"The doctor who came in with you? That was Dr. Hubble-Machado," the nurse said. Her English was really good; she had acted as translator for them since their arrival. "She's on the staff here. Lucky she was there, yes?" She pointed to a cord at the head of the bed. "The call button, you need something, okay?" She smiled at him and left the room.

"So what happened?" Dan asked.

Amy was relieved by the question. *Maybe he won't remember too much about it. What I remember is plenty enough for both of us.* She crossed her arms, trying to rub away the shivers brought on by the memory of seeing him lying there. . . .

Jake gave a quick rundown on the evil Mr. Blowpipe. "But here's the weird thing," he said. "I could have sworn that he was aiming at Atticus. *Not* Dan. It's almost like Dan was—you know, collateral damage."

Amy saw the expressions that flashed across Dan's face: surprise that he hadn't been the target, resentment that he'd been hit anyway, and finally, concern for Atticus, who was looking guilt-stricken now.

"No problem, Atticus," Dan said. "I've always wanted to be collateral damage."

Amy refused to joke about it. "You're sure you've never seen this guy before?" she said to Jake.

"No, but almost the whole time at the falls, I had the feeling someone was following us." He shook his head in distress. "I should have said something. But it probably wouldn't have made any difference, because it wasn't the blowpipe guy I was worried about."

"There was someone else?" Amy said.

"Yeah. Well, maybe." Jake looked confused.

"Just tell us what you saw," she snapped.

"I kept seeing the same person," he said. "But like I said, it wasn't the guy with the pipe. It was a woman."

"What did she look like?" Amy and Dan spoke at the same time.

"Taller than average. Pretty good-looking for someone her age—dark hair, sunglasses. Oh, and she was really well dressed. I remember that, because I thought it was a little weird to come to a place like this wearing such nice clothes."

Amy felt the blood draining from her face. Jake had just described someone the Cahills knew all too well.

Isabel Kabra.

Isabel.

A vial of the serum in one hand and a gun in the other, her fine features contorted by the ugliness of evil.

This was the image that first came to mind for Amy. Then, oddly, it was replaced almost at once by a memory of the female capoeirista: *"Um, dois, três—"*

Why? Why am I thinking about that now?

Like a radio being tuned from static to clarity, Amy could suddenly hear the capoeirista's next words. Her mouth went dry. She tried to swallow.

Not "more . . . a little less . . . a bell," but—

Amor to the littlest, from Isabel.

"It's definitely her," she said hoarsely. "And she's after Atticus."

CHAPTER 15

Nellie had always thought of herself as the tough and feisty type. Not aggressive or mean, but determined to achieve what she set out to do, loyal to those she loved, and fierce when it came to standing up for what she thought was right.

She was utterly unfamiliar with how she was feeling at the moment.

Defeated. Exhausted. Hopeless.

But that wasn't the worst of it. Try as she might, Nellie couldn't summon any anger. Since the moment she was kidnapped, she had been furious with the Vespers, and that fury had been like a flame inside her. Keeping her going, helping her keep the others going.

The flame had flickered out, extinguished by grief over the losses of Phoenix and Alistair.

I thought — I was sure — that somehow, we'd all get out of this alive.

Not that she hadn't been truly frightened any number of times. But deep down inside, it was in her nature as both a fighter and an optimist to expect good to prevail in the end.

Now she knew that, however this ended, Alistair and Phoenix would not be part of it.

Nellie looked around the room and saw her mood reflected in each of the others. Fiske lay stretched out on the floor, eyes closed most of the time. When they were open, he stared out into space, looking at nothing. Natalie sat with her back against a wall, her knees drawn up in a fetal position, hunched over and picking at her cuticles until they bled. Reagan was no longer working out. Instead she paced the bunker restlessly, prowling back and forth with no purpose, muttering to herself, driving them all crazy.

And Ted . . . well, it was hard to tell with Ted.

Because I can't look into his eyes. Nellie hadn't realized before spending all this time with Ted, how much she "read" people through the expressions in their eyes.

She looked at him now. He was sitting next to Natalie.

Huh — I can *read him. I can tell that he's not just sitting there. He's thinking — his brain is really working.*

Nellie walked over to Ted and sat down on the other side of him.

"I've remembered something," Ted said slowly. "The hiker. His voice — I was sure I'd heard it before, but I wasn't sure where at first."

He paused. Nellie felt her neck muscles tense up.

"And?" she prompted him. She clenched her fists

to stop herself from shaking Ted to knock the memory loose.

"Last summer I went out west with Sinead. She wanted to get away from everything. We stayed in the Olympic Mountains, in Washington State. We didn't do much, just hung out, went for some walks. It rained a lot, but that was okay—we didn't have any real plans.

"On one of the walks, we met this guy named Riley McGrath. I think Sinead kinda liked him. He invited us to go rock climbing, but I didn't want to go. She took me back to the lodge where we were staying and went on her own."

Ted turned his face toward Nellie.

"That's who the hiker was. Riley McGrath. So why would he say he was Martin Holds?"

Nellie tried to clear the fog of confusion from her brain. "Ted, are you sure? I mean, a lot of people's voices probably sound kind of alike—"

"Maybe to you," he said. "Not to me. Think of it this way. You might know two people who look similar, say, medium height, dark hair, average build, glasses. You can still tell them apart, right? No problem?"

"Sure."

"That's what it's like for me with voices. It was the same guy."

A tiny spark of hope ignited inside Nellie. She grabbed Ted's shoulder. "Maybe this tells us where we are! It could be a huge lead, Ted!"

Ted nodded slowly. "It's just too much of a coincidence, you know?"

Nellie got to her feet. "We've got to let Amy and Dan know somehow."

The only way to communicate with them was through the transmissions sent by the Vespers. Which were never sent for the convenience of the hostages.

With one hand in a fist, she punched her other palm several times. *Think. Think. Figure out a way to say it so they get the message. And then we'll just have to wait— I HATE all this waiting around!*

The spark inside her flared.

Nellie was mad again.

"She's after Atticus?" Dan and Jake said together at the same time that Atticus said, "Me—are you sure?"

The attack on Dan, followed immediately by the reappearance of Isabel: Amy felt her eyes getting hot, which meant tears were threatening to slither out yet again. She picked at the powder-burn blister on her neck, as if to provide an excuse if the tears did begin to fall. The blister was now turgid with fluid, like a tiny flattened water balloon.

Haltingly, she explained her theory. "*Um, dois, três.* One, two, three. I think it means that there will be three attacks. The first two have already happened. At the airport, and now this one."

A bubble of panic was growing in Amy's chest. *She's*

playing with us. Like a cat with a trapped mouse. There will be one more attack—the third. The final one . . .

"We have to get Atticus out of here!" She stood up so quickly that the chair fell over, her arms making jerky movements that she couldn't seem to control. "Jake, you take him to Attleboro on the next flight. That's the safest place for him. He'll have to stay there until—until all this is over. Once Dan recovers, we'll try to find Folio Seventy-four and join you there as soon as we can."

"I don't know," Jake said. "Wouldn't he be safer if we stuck together? You know, all three of us looking out for him? That way he—"

"HE is right next to you!" Atticus snapped. "Would you stop (A) treating me like a baby and (B) talking about me like I'm not here?! And for the record, I am NOT going somewhere to sit around and do nothing. Or take a *nap*." He glared at both of them.

"Atticus, you don't know her! She's completely, totally ruthless. The last time we were up against her, it took seven—no, *eight* of us to beat her." Amy was almost shrieking now. "Dan almost *died* just now. If anything happened to you—"

She had to stop talking because she couldn't get enough air into her lungs.

"I am NOT going to let anything happen to him—I mean, to you," Jake said, glancing quickly at Atticus. He turned a scowl on Amy. "What is your problem? Would you calm down—are you trying to scare him to death?"

"My problem?" Amy shouted. "My problem is, she almost killed my brother!"

"She knows what she's talking about," Dan said, entering the fray. "If you knew Isabel you'd be scared to death, too. I mean, look what she just did—" His hand went to his shoulder, and he winced as if the dart were still embedded there.

Atticus crossed his arms stubbornly. "This isn't just a Cahill thing anymore. It has something to do with Mom, and that makes it MY fight now just as much as it is yours. Maybe MORE. I'm not leaving until we know for sure whether the folio is here or not."

"Sorry, baby bro, not your call," Jake said.

"Why not?" Dan demanded. "Why can't he have a say in this?"

"Yeah, and quit calling me that!" Atticus said.

"Look, it's my responsibility—"

"STOP IT! STOP STOP STOP!"

All three boys stared at Amy in shock. In the sudden silence, she could hear herself breathing. Gasping.

"Think," she whispered to herself. "Think think think . . ."

But there was no room in her head for anything except fear, and she didn't notice the worried glances exchanged by the boys.

After a few moments, Dan spoke carefully. "Amy," he said. "I agree with Jake—that it's riskier to send the two of them back than it is to stay together. Besides, it won't be for very long. I mean, the deadline—we'll all be going back soon, one way or the other."

Somebody else making the decision. On the one hand, it was exactly what Amy wanted at that moment. On the other, it felt terrible — weak, indecisive, and unworthy of the trust Grace had bestowed on her.

Just this once, Grace.

"Okay," she mumbled.

The sense of relief that the four of them would be staying together lasted about half a second. Then the dread returned.

Um, dois, três . . .

Dan insisted that he felt fine and wanted to leave the hospital. The doctor on call refused to sign the release form, saying that the patient needed to stay overnight for observation.

After the doctor was gone, Dan looked at the others. "I can't stay overnight," he said. "We don't have time for that."

A noisy discussion ensued, which boiled down to Dan vs. Amy with the Rosenblooms refereeing. When the nurse came in, they all fell silent, but then Amy asked her a few questions, and the nurse assured her that the overnight stay was just a precaution. She took Dan's pulse and temperature.

"You are healthy as *um cavalo* — horse," she said cheerfully. "The young ones, they bounce quick, very good!" She left the room again.

More fuel for Dan's side of the argument. Finally, Atticus looked up curare poisoning online and found enough information to convince Amy—and himself, Dan thought—that it would be okay for Dan to leave the hospital.

Amy may not be happy about it, but she knows we have to do this, Dan thought as he hopped out of bed and got dressed.

The foursome had no choice but to sneak away when the nurse's back was turned. They caught a taxi outside the hospital.

"I hope she doesn't get in trouble for this," Dan said, meaning the nurse. "She was really nice."

Dan's left arm still seemed a little fuzzy, but otherwise he felt great. He wished Amy would stop fussing over him. She had made him zip his jacket all the way up to his chin. Like that made any difference, except to make him look totally uncool. At the same time, he knew she *needed* to fuss over him, so he tried to keep the sighs and eye-rolls to a minimum.

"Now, where were we?" he asked.

Their mission seemed a lifetime away, but they had to click back into search mode. "The folio," Atticus said. "We were going to search underneath the walkway, remember?"

"Any climbing stuff, you're out of the picture," Amy said to Dan. "And don't even try to talk me out of it."

"Rope, harnesses, some carabiner clips," Jake said.

"A sporting-goods store would be our best bet. Second best, a hardware store."

"Anyone know how to say *carabiner clips* in Portuguese?" Dan asked. "Didn't think so."

He booted up his laptop. "I'll find an online translator," he said. "Then maybe the driver can help us."

One of the Voynich images was now his home page. It was Folio 75 — the "plumbing picture." He clicked on the browser icon, and the screen filled with the image of basins overflowing with water and naked women.

Next to him, the driver glanced over. "Ah," he said with a grin. *"Mabu, sim?"*

Dan looked at him blankly. The driver pointed to the image on the screen.

"Isto é Mabu," he said firmly. "Mabu."

Whatever the guy was saying, he seemed really sure about it. Dan spoke on impulse. "Okay, Mabu. Let's go — *vámonos.*"

Which was Spanish, not Portuguese, but the driver got the message and pulled away from the curb, tires squealing.

The backseat reacted immediately. "Whoa!" "What's going on?" "Where are we going?"

Dan explained about the driver's reaction to the Voynich image. "He seems to think it's something called Mabu," he said. "So I told him to take us there."

"That's ridiculous!" Amy said. "You have no idea what he's talking about — it could be hundreds of miles away!"

"It might not be a place," Jake pointed out. "Mabu could be a person. A famous swimmer, maybe."

Atticus's eyes were as round as CDs. "What if it's, like, a nudist colony?"

Dan snorted. "You wish."

"We don't have time to waste on wild-goose chases," Amy said. "Stop this nonsense and ask him for a sporting-goods store."

"It might not be far," Dan countered. "What's the harm in checking it out?"

They were still arguing a few minutes later when the taxi turned into a driveway that led to a big hotel.

"Mabu," the driver said with a satisfied expression.

The sign said MABU THERMAS HOTEL AND SPA.

"'Hotel and Spa'—it could still be for nudists, couldn't it?" Atticus said. "Gimme the laptop." He took it from Dan and began tapping on the keyboard.

Amy was sitting like a stone, refusing to move. Dan opened the taxi door. "Come on, Amy—"

"No—YOU come on! Some random guy takes us to a random hotel, and you think it could be part of this?"

Her voice, shrill and brittle, was setting off alarm bells in Dan's head. *Why is she acting like this? Okay, so she doesn't think it's a great idea, but does she have to get hysterical about it?*

Amy's shrieking continued. "I can't believe—you can't possibly—"

"Hey!" Atticus cut her off with a grin and held up the laptop. "Poos!"

CHAPTER 16

The hotel's pools were its most famous feature. According to the website, an underground thermal spring bubbled up into a large hot tub. It was constructed so the water would spill out via a waterfall into a swimming pool built on a lower level. The water in the pool cascaded into yet another pool, with the temperature getting cooler with each successive level; you could choose whether to simmer in the hot tub or be refreshed in the lowest pool.

Atticus smacked himself on the head. "The word *pools* in Dr. Siffright's message—that should have told us it couldn't possibly be the big falls." He bounced up and down a little. "I have a feeling—this could be the right place!"

With Amy partly mollified, the group checked in and went to their rooms. None of them had swimming gear, so the boys all put on shorts. Amy had to go to the hotel shop to find a bathing suit, her companions helpfully trailing along.

Atticus pulled a suit off the rack. "How does this

even *work*?" he said, examining it in wonder. Several skinny black straps were connected in a complicated and mysterious way to a few tiny triangles of fabric.

"I believe it's called a thong," Jake said wisely.

Amy blushed, snatched it away from Atticus, and hung it back up on the rack. "I am *not* wearing that."

"Amy, how about this one?" Dan held a spangly leopard-print number under his chin and sashayed a few steps, wiggling his hips.

"Oh, Dan, that's *so* you!" Jake said in falsetto. All three boys howled with laughter.

"Would you all please just LEAVE?" Amy said, now bright pink with mortification.

"Okay, okay," Jake said, his hands raised in mock surrender. "We'll wait outside."

A few minutes later, Amy joined them wearing a towel wrapped around her waist and a navy-blue striped bikini. They took the elevator down to the pool level. As they pushed through the glass doors, Atticus put one hand over his eyes and peeked through his fingers.

"Not nudist," he announced, and Jake could hear the relief in his voice.

About a dozen other people were in the pools, with a handful more lounging in deck chairs on the extensive patio. Jake moved a little closer to Amy.

"What's the plan?" he asked, his voice low.

He followed her gaze as she looked around. The hot tub, two big pools, the patio . . . There was a lot of ground to cover.

She didn't answer, so he went on, "We can start with this pool, it's the biggest. Atticus, you and Dan take the perimeter. Amy and I will search the rest of it."

"Is that an order?" Amy said and crossed her arms over her chest. "Or just a suggestion?"

"I'm only trying to help," Jake said. "And Atticus, you don't go anywhere on your own. One of us always has to be next to you, understand?"

Atticus seemed about to talk back, but Jake's expression clearly indicated zero tolerance on this. With a shrug, he cannonballed into the pool, followed immediately by Dan.

Amy was watching Dan. Her expression seemed to soften a little; Dan already appeared free of any effects from the curare.

She cleared her throat and turned to Jake. "We should try not to look like we're searching," she said.

"Agreed." Jake thought for a moment. "Can you swim the butterfly stroke?"

"Yes," she said, "not great. But why—"

"I can't," he said. "So you can teach me. That'll be our cover for going back and forth across the pool a million times."

"Good idea," she said.

Which felt almost as good as making her laugh.

"I don't get it," Dan said to Atticus as they inspected the perimeter of the first pool. "If it's a manuscript page we're looking for, a swimming pool would be the worst place to hide it, right? If it got wet, it could be ruined forever."

Atticus thought for a moment. "Yeah, but maybe that's why she hid it here. Because no one would think of looking for it in a pool."

"I don't know," Dan said, shaking his head. "Even if she wrapped it up really good, it seems like an awfully big risk."

Atticus scanned the whole area carefully. "Maybe you're right," he said slowly. "How about this: *near* the pool, but not *in* it?"

They climbed out of the pool.

"You start here and I'll start over there," Dan said, pointing toward the outer edge of the patio area. "We can meet in the middle." He headed for the fence that bordered the patio.

Atticus decided that searching the permanent structures first made the most sense. Surely Dr. Siffright wouldn't have hidden the manuscript page under something like a lounge chair or patio table that could easily be moved.

A few yards from the pool, there was a hut for towel storage. It wasn't much more than a wooden counter beneath a palm-frond roof. Clean folded towels were stacked on one end of the counter; at the other end, a rectangular hole had been cut into the wood, with a rolling laundry bin underneath.

Atticus walked to the hut to begin his search, then

took a quick glance around. Jake and Amy were still checking out the pool. Dan was examining the wrought-iron fence. Atticus didn't see anything suspect, but just in case . . .

He reached for a towel and began drying himself.

"Oh, that feels good!" he said loudly and wiped his legs and arms with exaggerated motions. As a final flourish, he draped the towel around his neck. *That should throw off anyone who might be spying,* he thought with satisfaction.

Atticus searched the little hut thoroughly. *I have to find the folio. Dan got hurt because of me.*

He even moved the laundry bin so he could inspect the floor space underneath.

Nothing.

He rolled the laundry bin back into its place under the counter. As he straightened up, his glance fell on one of the bamboo poles supporting the roof of the hut. He followed it with his gaze to the palm fronds overhead.

What if it's hidden up there?

Skinny bamboo poles and palm fronds. The roof would never support his weight.

A ladder . . . where am I going to get a ladder? And even if I can find one, it would look awfully strange, me climbing up to get a look at the roof. . . .

Atticus decided to consult Dan on this one. He looked toward the fence, but Dan wasn't there.

Jake and Amy in the pool, check. Where's Dan?

He surveyed the patio area carefully.

Still no Dan.

Atticus started to feel a little knot of panic in his stomach. *What if he's, like, passed out because—because of the curare affecting him somehow?* He looked around one more time.

The knot loosened. *There he is!*

Not far from the fence, Dan was on his hands and knees on the ground; that was why Atticus hadn't spotted him at first. Dan seemed to be talking to a woman standing near him. She was wearing sunglasses and a floppy hat.

Something about the way she's standing . . . Atticus couldn't have said exactly what it was, but the woman looked tense to him. Then he realized that, although her arms were down by her sides, her right hand was clenched around something.

She took a step toward Dan, and the object in her hand flashed in the sunlight.

Atticus gasped.

A knife!

Dan had spent only a few minutes searching the wrought-iron fence. He didn't see how the manuscript page could be hidden there, unless it was buried at the base of one of the pilings, which were set into concrete. He decided instead to search the patio itself, which had sections of both brickwork and wood decking.

Determined to do a thorough job of it, Dan went down to his hands and knees and began to crawl around the patio. He knew it looked strange, but he could always reprise the contact-lens excuse if anyone asked.

The wood planking was solid and the bricks well mortared, but where they met, there was a seam that formed the narrowest of cracks. Dan fingered the crack experimentally. *You could fit something down there, all right,* he thought. *It would be awfully tight, but maybe the crack is wider somewhere else—if I follow it along . . .*

He turned to begin tracing the path of the crack. Out of the corner of his eye, he saw movement and looked up.

And up, and up.

A woman was standing nearby. She was really tall—it was hard to tell from Dan's vantage point, but she had to be at least six feet. Sunglasses, straw hat, one of those terry-cloth swim cover-ups.

"What are you doing?" she said in a voice not much louder than a whisper.

Dan glanced around quickly, then back at the woman. "Sorry—were you talking to me?" he asked. His heart was starting to beat a little harder. "I just—I'm—um—"

The woman took a small step toward him. "Get away from there," she said in a voice so tight she was almost choking. "Just stand up and walk away. I don't want to hurt you, but I will if I have to." She made a small motion with her right hand.

Dan looked at her hand and saw part of a knife's blade. He got to his knees slowly.

The woman glanced around, then took a couple of steps. She was now standing behind him.

"Get up," she said.

Dan felt the chill of metal against his neck. Cold sweat broke out all over his body. It felt like even his elbows were sweating. And why did his left arm suddenly feel a lot weaker?

"Hey, Dan!"

Atticus was waving at him. The woman stayed where she was but lowered the knife out of sight. It pressed between Dan's shoulder blades.

"Wanna go in again?" Atticus was all smiles. "Bet I can hold my breath underwater longer than you—c'mon—" He started trotting toward Dan.

"Get rid of him," the woman croaked.

Atticus was now just steps away. Dan felt the knife twitch against his skin. Sweat was rolling down his back—or was it blood?

Could I elbow her, maybe? But she's on my left—is my arm strong enough for that?

"Atticus, um, I want a Coke," Dan said in desperation. "Would you go to the bar and get me one? Right now? Like, right this minute? I'm *really* thirsty."

Atticus, LISTEN to me, go on, get away from here!

To his utter amazement, Atticus gave him a subtle, secret thumbs-up.

Then Atticus leaped to the woman's side, grabbed the towel from around his neck, and flicked it like a whip at her hand. She cried out in pain and dropped the knife; it clattered to the ground, bounced, and ended up not far from Dan. She and Dan both dove for the knife.

Dan got there first. His fingers closed around the handle—

"HEY!"

It was Jake's voice, followed immediately by Amy's. "DAN, ATTICUS! RUN!"

Atticus turned instantly to obey, but in his haste he tripped on the towel, knocked down a small table, and plowed into a lounge chair. The chair landed on its side; both Dan and the woman fell over it.

The towel ended up half draped over Dan's head. One of Atticus's hands was trapped in the chair's plastic webbing. The woman's hat had been knocked off and her sunglasses were askew.

It was her voice that emerged first from the pile.

"Atticus?" she said. "Atticus Rosenbloom?"

Atticus stared at her for a moment.

"Dr. Siffright?"

CHAPTER 17

Disentanglement was followed by multiple explanations.

"Atticus isn't a common name," Dr. Siffright said. "And you're the right age, and now I can see it—you look like Astrid."

"I hope I didn't hurt your hand," Atticus said. "I didn't know it was you."

"You didn't stay with Dan," Jake said to Atticus. "I *told* you—"

"I forgot," Atticus confessed. "It's hard to remember every single minute."

"If you forget again, I'm putting you on a leash," Jake said. Then he relented a little. "That was really brave, what you did. Weren't you scared?"

"Yeah," Atticus admitted. "I *was* scared, but I was more scared for Dan."

Dan was still holding the knife. Now he looked at it more closely. It was a butter knife, like a small paddle.

"You were going to attack me with *this*?" he said, incredulous.

Dr. Siffright reddened. "I just grabbed whatever was handy," she said. "I didn't—I wasn't—I mean, this is *not* my usual line of work." She shrugged, then lowered her head sheepishly. "To be honest, I was shaking the whole time. But look, we have a lot to talk about. Why don't we all get changed and meet in the restaurant?"

The hotel's restaurant was a *churrascaria*, serving Brazilian-style barbecue. Amy, Dan, and Jake scanned the place quickly, then Jake asked for a table in the corner, in an empty part of the room. Amy knew what he was thinking: This way, they would easily be able to see the rest of the room and anyone approaching them. At the table, Dr. Siffright sat between Jake and Atticus, with Amy and Dan opposite.

Amy thought the *churrascaria* was one of the coolest places she'd ever eaten at. First, they all served themselves at the appetizer buffet, which was at least thirty feet long and held everything from salads to sushi. Ordinary things—lettuce, tomatoes, cheese cubes—alternated with exotic offerings like hearts of palm and manioc.

After they were finished with their appetizers, Dr. Siffright picked up a flat disk by her plate. Each of them had one; they were about the size of coasters, with one side red and the other green.

"You put this by your plate with the green side up when you want meat," she explained. "If you don't want any more, you flip it over to the red side."

Five green disks went faceup on the table. Immediately waiters swarmed around, carrying giant skewers filled with grilled meat. The skewers were easily three feet long, and each waiter held a knife the size of a machete.

"Chicken," said the first waiter. "You like some chicken?"

"I have sirloin steak here."

"Anybody want lamb chops?"

"Wow," Jake said, his eyes wide. "I think we took a wrong turn. We're supposed to be in Brazil, but this seems more like heaven to me."

"Meat heaven," Dan agreed.

Amy had to laugh at them; they were practically panting. "Swallow, all of you," she said to the boys, "before the whole table gets flooded with drool."

The waiters carved chicken and lamb onto Amy's plate. Atticus took a little of everything, and Jake and Dan took a *lot* of everything.

The meat was delicious: charred and smoky outside, tender and juicy within. It had been ages since they'd taken the time to have a really good meal.

The waiters came around again, this time with sausages and bacon-wrapped shrimp. With each new wave of meat, the noises of appreciation made by the boys became less coherent. *Another serving or two and they'll all be grunting like cavemen,* Amy thought.

With the deep sweet taste of a grilled red pepper

in her mouth, Amy realized that for the last twenty minutes, she hadn't thought of Isabel or the Vespers. She'd been thinking of nothing but food.

Instant guilt. Lots of it. Enough so that the pepper suddenly turned dry and savorless.

She made a silent deal with herself: *No guilt until I'm done eating. Then it's back to work.* Her heart sank at the thought, so she took a bite of shrimp to cheer herself up.

They were all too busy eating to talk much, except to comment on the food. At last Amy looked up from her plate. Before she could even take a breath, another waiter had rushed over.

"Ribeye? I have ribeye here, very delicious."

Amy held her hands up. "No, thank you. Really— I can't eat another bite."

"Flip your disk over," Dr. Siffright suggested.

Amy complied. Dr. Siffright's disk was already red-side up, and Amy noticed that she had eaten very little of what was on her plate. Dr. Siffright sat still except for her hands, which kept twiddling with her napkin.

The boys stayed in the game for one more round of skewers. Eventually Amy saw the pace of their forks begin to falter.

"Disks to red?" she said. She glanced at Dr. Siffright. "So no one will bother us for a while and we can talk."

Dr. Siffright nodded as the boys flipped their disks. "Okay," she said quietly. "Who wants to go first?"

It was hard to know where to start. After a few moments of uneasy silence, Amy prompted Jake to talk about Astrid's interest in the Voynich and their recent trip to Yale.

"You went because of your mom?" Dr. Siffright asked.

"No, not exactly." Jake looked at Amy for help.

Amy hesitated.

"It's okay, Amy," Atticus said. "Mom trusted her, so we should, too."

Dr. Siffright stiffened. "Actually, the real question is whether *I* can trust *you*."

Amy made up her mind quickly. She looked Dr. Siffright in the eye. "I'm sorry," she said. "What Atticus meant was, we're in trouble and we need your help. This is probably going to sound crazy, but our friends have been kidnapped. . . ."

With the three boys chipping in occasionally, Amy laid out the whole mess with the Vespers. Dr. Siffright listened without interrupting, intent but expressionless, pulling at a thread in her napkin.

When at last they were finished, a shroud of silence fell over the table. Amy waited as long as she could, then finally spoke.

"I know it sounds unbelievable," she said, "but every word is the truth. If we don't give Folio Seventy-four to the Vespers, one of our friends will die."

Dr. Siffright frowned, clearly deep in thought. "I do

believe you," she said. "At least, I think I do. Actually, what you've said explains a lot."

It was her turn now. "About a year and a half ago, I went to Italy. Like many people who learn about the Voynich, I'd become obsessed. I gave up trying to decode it, but I still want to know as much as I can about it. I decided to see if I could find any of the missing folios."

Dr. Siffright went on to explain that she had indeed located a mysterious manuscript page. "I found it in a monastery—not the one where Voynich found the original manuscript, but a different one. They had hundreds of boxes, files, chests—all filled with old manuscripts. It took me months to comb through them."

"And they let you take it?" Atticus asked.

Dr. Siffright smiled wanly. "For a price. Let's just say, I live in a small apartment these days. I had to sell my house to get enough money to buy it."

Amy resisted the urge to glance at her other tablemates. *She sold her house for it?! What Dr. James said about her—intense and single-minded when it comes to the Voynich—that sounds like an understatement now.*

"It turns out someone else wanted it, too," Dr. Siffright said. "Although I didn't know that at first. I brought the folio back and began the process of authentication. I didn't tell Yale or anyone else about it. I didn't want to broadcast the fact that I had it, because if it proved not to be genuine, my reputation as a scholar could have been damaged."

She was now twisting the napkin in earnest. "I'd been home for a few weeks when I started noticing strange things. First my car was broken into. And my apartment — twice. At work, they sent out a notice that several e-mail accounts at Brown had been hacked.

"Worst of all, I started to suspect that someone was following me. I asked myself a hundred times a day if it was real or if I was just being paranoid."

She looked from Jake to Atticus and back again. "Astrid was the only person I could talk to about this. In fact, she said that similar things were happening to her, and like me, she thought it might be just her imagination."

Amy saw the dismay on the faces of both Jake and Atticus as they exchanged glances.

"She never said anything to us," Jake said.

"I wish we'd known!" Atticus said in distress. "Maybe we could have helped somehow — " He stopped, tears filling his eyes. He wiped them away angrily with his sleeve.

"She probably didn't want to worry you," Dr. Siffright said.

"That would be . . . like her," Jake said, his voice catching a little.

Amy felt their pain in the pit of her stomach. *It's bad enough when someone you love dies. But to think that they were afraid before they died . . .* She remembered the panic in Dan's eyes when he was lying on the ground, and picked at the blister on her neck again. She knew she shouldn't — it was getting irritated — but her hand kept going there of its own accord.

Dr. Siffright reached out to touch Atticus's arm. "She wasn't alone in this," she said gently. "We were helping each other through it."

Jake nodded. "Thanks," he said.

After a moment, Dr. Siffright went on. "Astrid suggested that I hide the page somewhere very secure. At the time I had already booked a trip to Brazil — I love it, I've been here many times. So I brought the page with me and hid it here. It's so remote — I thought it would be safe. But because I felt like I was being followed, I decided to let Astrid know where it was, just in case" — she paused — "anything happened to me."

"That's how we found you," Atticus said. "The coded e-mails."

Dr. Siffright smiled. "Nice job," she said. "That tells me you're Astrid's kids for sure."

"And we had help from Dr. James," Jake said, "at Yale."

"You met Kathryn?" Dr. Siffright said. "Did she tell you I was crazy?" She laughed softly. "No, she wouldn't, she's too polite. But I know she thinks I am." She paused. "The line between passionate and crazy can be a thin one. Maybe she's right. I mean, here I am, guarding a piece of paper for months. . . ."

Dr. Siffright shrugged, then went on. "So, from what you're telling me, if I wasn't imagining things, then it's the Vespers who've been following me."

"And broke into your apartment and tried to hack your e-mail," Dan said. "It sounds like exactly the sort of things they'd do."

Dr. Siffright looked at Dan apologetically. "By the way, that's why I pulled the knife on you," she said. "I thought maybe you were part of — of whoever was following me."

Dan shrugged. "I'd have done the same," he said, then grinned. "But I'd have picked a way better knife."

Amy decided that the conversation had gone on long enough. "Will you help us, Dr. Siffright? Will you give us the manuscript page? I promise that if there's anything I can do to get it back to you, I will."

Silence followed. Tension stiffened Amy's shoulders; Dr. Siffright looked like she was about to make a decision. *And if it's no, it'll be final. She won't change her mind.*

A waiter was approaching the table. Their disks were still red-side up, but he came closer anyway, smiling broadly.

Amy felt a flare of annoyance. *Not now,* she thought. *Don't bother us now. All the other waiters have left us alone — can't you see that our disks are red?*

As she picked up her disk to show him the red side, the thought echoed in her mind: *All the other waiters have left us alone. . . .*

Amy screamed before she had even finished the thought.

"ATTICUS!"

CHAPTER 18

The waiter's smile contorted into a terrible leer. He whipped the huge knife off the tray and hurled it at Atticus; in the next split second, the knife was followed by the skewer.

Dr. Siffright reacted so quickly that it seemed like Amy's scream was still reverberating. She threw her six-foot-plus frame in front of Atticus. Together they crashed to the floor when Atticus's chair tipped over backward.

Amy, Dan, and Jake leapt to their feet. Jake went for the waiter, who flung the tray at him. The tray conked Jake squarely in the face and spattered hot meat drippings in his eyes; he staggered back, yelping in pain.

Meanwhile, Dan and Amy scrambled to the other side of the table, tripping over the chairs in their haste.

Dan's eyes widened. There was blood everywhere. Atticus lay on the floor, eyes closed and his body so limp that he had to be—

Unconscious, Dan thought, *please please let him be unconscious and not—*

"Dan!" Jake shouted. "The waiter!"

Dan looked up just in time to see the doors to the kitchen swing closed. A noise that was half growl, half shout rose from Dan's throat as he ran toward the kitchen.

Bad timing: Dan burst through the swinging doors right into a full cadre of skewer-bearing waiters. With a deafening clatter, Dan ended up on the floor amid the debris of a mini-explosion: skewers, trays, knives, grilled meat, and very angry waiters.

Dan got up and tried to continue the pursuit, but slipped on a pork chop and fell again. He pounded his fist on the floor in frustration.

Too late. Whoever he is, he's got a big head start by now.

Ignoring outraged protests from the other waiters, Dan hurried back to the dining room. A crowd had gathered around their table.

"Atticus?" he said, his voice hoarse with strain. "Atticus! Let me through, you idiots!" He shouldered, elbowed, and kneed people out of his way.

Dan was nearly sick with relief when he saw Atticus sitting up, supported by Jake. "He's okay," Jake said. "The skewer got him in the earlobe—a lot of blood, but no real damage. Go help Amy!"

The knife had sliced into Dr. Siffright's neck.

"Get me another napkin," Amy said tersely. She was applying pressure to Dr. Siffright's wound with a napkin already soaked in blood.

Dan grabbed two clean napkins from an unoccupied table. He handed them to Amy, then knelt down next to her. Dr. Siffright's face had turned so white it was almost blue; her eyes were glazed and unfocused.

"Did somebody call 9-1-1?" Dan asked.

As if in response, he heard sirens outside. A few minutes later, a team of paramedics rushed into the restaurant.

Dan and Amy relinquished their places to the EMTs. Working quickly but gently, they applied a pressure bandage to Dr. Siffright's neck and loaded her onto a gurney.

As they prepared to wheel her out, a paramedic bent over Dr. Siffright, then straightened and looked around.

"Dan? Is there someone here named Dan? She wants to talk to you."

Dan rushed to the gurney. He leaned over so he could hear the weak thread of words coming from Dr. Siffright's pale lips.

"You know," she whispered. "You . . . you know . . ."

Then to Dan's horror, her eyes rolled back in her head and she slipped into unconsciousness.

Hours later, the four friends sat on the beds in Amy and Dan's hotel room. They had all been questioned by the police. None of the restaurant staff knew who the "waiter" was; he had been wearing the right uniform, no one had even really noticed him. The police had concluded that the attack was most likely a random act by an unbalanced individual.

Unbalanced — not exactly the word Dan would have used to describe the Vespers. *More like loony to the nth degree.*

Dr. Siffright was in intensive care, no visitors allowed. When they called, the doctor would only say that Dr. Siffright had lost a lot of blood and they would have to wait and see how she responded to treatment.

Atticus was gingerly fingering the tape on his earlobe; a paramedic on the scene had cleaned up the cut and bandaged it. Jake too had been treated, with ointment on the superficial burns on his face. Dan thought Atticus was in the best shape of the four of them. It turned out that Atticus, to his eternal embarrassment, had fainted when the skewer hit. The assault had happened so quickly that it seemed the danger hadn't really sunk in for him.

Jake was pacing the room in a boil of fury and self-blame. "I let my guard down," he said. "I was all relaxed — the food was so good and we were talking and I wasn't alert —"

"Cut it out," Dan said. "There's no use blaming yourself. We have to figure out what to do next."

Everyone looked at Amy, who avoided their glances and seemed preoccupied with the blister on her neck. When she finally did speak, her voice was a faded copy of itself.

"We've got nothing," she said. Dan saw her glance at her watch; even that small normal act was a reminder of their burdens, with the Madrigal ring embedded in the dial's casing. "And as long as Dr. Siffright can't have any visitors, we can't get anything more from her."

"We could try sneaking in," Jake suggested. "I could dress up as — as a janitor, maybe, and try to get into her room to talk to her."

"Wait." Atticus did a little butt-bounce on the bed and turned to Dan. "She said something to you — right before they took her away, didn't she?"

"Yeah, but it was hardly anything," Dan said. "She passed out really fast."

"But what did she say?" Atticus insisted.

Dan frowned. "She didn't get to it," he said. "She was just starting to say something — she said, 'You know —' and that was it."

"That's all?" Amy asked. "Are you sure?"

Dan made a helpless shrug and saw Amy's shoulders sag even lower. "She said it twice. 'You know, you know.' Does that help?" he said, his voice bitter with disappointment.

"Actually, maybe it does," Atticus said. "What if she wasn't saying, 'you know,' the way you do when it doesn't mean anything, but it was more like, 'You know.' I mean, she did ask for *you*, specifically. Maybe you know something the rest of us don't."

"What could I know? I only just met her!" Dan said.

Now Jake was sitting up straighter, too. "Try the visualization thing," he suggested, "from when you first saw her."

"But I didn't even know who she was then! And besides, you all got there, like, a couple seconds later—"

Dan stopped. As soon as Jake had said "visualization," his mind had immediately clicked back to the swimming-pool patio. He had been on his hands and knees—Dr. Siffright had said something—what had she said? *"Get away from there."*

From where?

"The crack!" he shouted. "I was looking at the crack—" He jumped to his feet and headed for the door.

"What crack?" the other three said all together, as if they'd rehearsed the timing.

"Never mind—just come on!" Dan yelled.

The pools were lit, glowing a brilliant turquoise. The patio area was mostly dark. No one was in either pool, but there were a few people enjoying the hot tub.

Dan led the group to the point near the fence where the wood decking met the brickwork.

"I was right around here somewhere," he said, his voice low.

"Flashlight app," Jake said, and they all pulled their phones out of their pockets.

"Spread out," Dan said.

The crack was not a straight line. It curved artistically in loose S-shapes. At arm's-width distance from each other, they began their search.

Less than a minute later, Dan called out softly to the

others. "I can see something," he said. It made sense; it was very close to where he'd been searching when Dr. Siffright threatened him with the butter knife.

Three other cell phones joined his, shining light into the narrow crack.

"I see it!" Atticus said excitedly.

The object was only an inch or two below the surface, but the opening was way too small for their fingers, even Atticus's.

"Easy enough to drop it in there," Jake said, "but how was she going to get it out? There's no way *her* fingers would have fit, either."

Amy stood up. "I'll be right back," she said and ran into the hotel.

"Um." Atticus looked at the other two boys with his eyebrows raised. "That was kind of—sudden."

Jake turned to Dan. "Should one of us go after her?"

Dan considered for a moment. "Let's give her a minute," he said. *She wasn't upset. No, that's not right, she's always upset these days. But she seemed okay.* He hoped he was reading her right.

The boys began discussing the possibility of removing some of the deck's wood planks.

"These three boards," Jake said, drawing his finger across the wood. "We could take out the nails with a hammer, and then pry them up. It'll take a while—we'll have to do it in the middle of the night."

"We'll need a saw, too," Dan said. "It'd be a lot easier to pry up a shorter length of board, wouldn't it?"

"But that might make a lot of noise," Atticus pointed out. "I think early in the morning would be better—before people want to swim, but late enough so maybe they'll think the noise is construction or something."

"I don't know," Jake said. "If anyone sees us, what excuse could we give for tearing up the patio?"

"We can't buy the tools until the shops open in the morning," Dan said. "We'll have to do it in broad daylight."

"Looks like that's our only option," Jake said grimly. "So let's make a list. Hammer, saw—what kind of saw would be best? And how about a crowbar, that might help—"

"A crowbar?" It was Amy, approaching them with her toiletries bag. "I don't think so. Could you give me a little light here?"

Jake directed a flashlight-app beam at the toiletries bag. Dan looked at Amy quizzically. "You have a zit emergency?" he asked.

Amy fished out what she was looking for. "Let's not do a demolition job until we try this first," she said and held out her hand.

Tweezers.

CHAPTER 19

The tweezers worked. With Amy doing the honors, tugging first at one corner then the other, a sturdy sheet of laminated plastic emerged from the crack.

Back in the hotel room, everyone gathered around to examine their find.

Dr. Siffright had put Folio 74 inside a clear plastic folder. Then the folder had been laminated—not in the standard school or home-office way, but heavy-duty, with sealed edges identical to those used in the packaging of electronic devices.

"Wow, she was smart," Atticus said. "It's like when you buy a calculator or something—those packages are always *impossible* to open."

"Kept it nice and dry, and you don't even need to open it to see both sides," Dan added.

One side of the folio was covered with line after line of the instantly recognizable handwriting in "Voynichese." But there was no use spending any time on the un-decodable lines, so she turned the sheet of plastic over.

On the other side was a beautiful and elaborate drawing of three astronomical circles. Similar to those they had seen previously in the manuscript, the circles appeared to indicate phases of different celestial bodies, possibly the sun, the earth, and the moon.

"They're not the same as the other ones," Dan said immediately. Amy recognized the authority in his voice; she knew he was accessing the photographic-memory part of his brain.

"For one thing, these mesh together. None of the other circles did that. And none of them had these teeth." Dan pointed to the edges of one of the circles.

A row of perfect triangles rimmed each circle.

"They're gears!" Jake exclaimed.

"So it's some kind of machine?" Dan said.

Atticus picked up the encased folio and peered at it closely. "There's something else here," he said slowly. "Maybe . . . pencil that somebody tried to erase."

He pointed to a space just above where two of the circles overlapped, then handed the folio to Amy.

The page showed the variations in color and texture typical of ancient vellum: old crease marks, crackling, patches of uneven hues.

Amy shifted her position so the light from the over-head lamp fell on the page more directly, and held it a little closer.

"I see it now," she said.

Above the intersection of two of the circles was a very faint line leading to an even fainter figure — a simple five-pointed star.

Amy handed the folio to Dan, who put it down on the bed and took out his phone. Using the flashlight app again, he went over the page thoroughly.

"There's more," he said slowly. "Same thing — pencil that's been erased. I think it's . . . two words, and one of them's pretty clear. A-N-T-I-K, *antik*."

"Maybe whoever wrote it couldn't spell *antique*?" Jake guessed.

Dan frowned. "The other word is written smaller. And kind of smudged."

Amy dug into her toiletries bag again. "Try this." She handed him a magnifying mirror.

"What do girls need all that stuff for?" Atticus asked, sounding half admiring and half mystified.

Holding the mirror at an angle in front of the page, Dan spelled out the letters one by one. "H," he said. "Then O — or it could be a C. And then a P — no, wait, I think it's an R, not a P. And then A."

Jake grabbed a pen and pad from the nightstand. "H-O-R-A," he repeated as he wrote the letters down.

"Hora," Amy said. "That means 'hour' in Spanish, or it could mean 'time,' too. Well, they're astronomical charts, duh — of course they have something to do with time. Hora, antique — it's not a clue, it's just someone's useless scribbling." Amy knew she sounded snarky, but she couldn't help it.

Atticus was frowning. "H-O-R-A . . . but that's backward!" he said. He nudged Dan.

"You were reading from the reflection, so it's backward. It's really, um, let's see—"

He was sitting across from Jake and had to read the letters on the pad upside down. "—A-R-O-H."

"Which could mean anything," Amy said crossly.

"Wait," Dan said. "What if it's a C instead of an O—"

"A-R-C-H—arch!" Jake shouted.

Jake and Dan immediately began a game of verbal ping-pong.

"St. Louis—the Gateway Arch."

"The Arc de Triomphe in Paris."

"Arches National Park."

Amy listened to their conversation without really hearing it. She knew she should be contributing, or at least trying to. But after the high from the successful use of her tweezers idea, she was coming down hard now. A strange feeling had been growing in her—since Erasmus's death? Or Phoenix's? She wasn't sure when it had begun, but she had gradually become more aware of it, and now it could no longer be ignored.

It was as if her mind was slowly dividing into two parts. One part of her was leading the boys around the planet to battle the Vespers, in a constant state of adrenaline-fueled anxiety, tension, and desperation. The other part was like a spectator, or a passenger maybe, detached, uninvolved—and uncaring.

That part of her had begun to feel like a safe place.

No Vespers. No Isabel. No menacing capoeiristas or assassins disguised as waiters. A place in her mind that was quiet because it was empty.

As hard as she tried to fight off the impulse, Amy found herself wanting to go there more and more often.

"Amy?" It was Dan, dragging her out of her thoughts. "Arches—what's the first thing you think of?"

"McDonald's," she said automatically.

"Very funny," Jake said. "Come on, we're making progress, get in here and help."

He reached out and pulled her into the huddle. His hand on her arm was warm. . . .

Unbidden, the image of Evan's face popped into her head. Why was she thinking of him now? Why did everything have to be so complicated?

Then Atticus made a gesture: one hand making a quick arc that ended with a snap of his fingers.

"Snap," he said. "I've got it. *Arch* isn't an arch."

His voice was quiet, but they could all hear the certainty in it.

"Okay," Jake said. "So what is it, then?"

"It's a person. Archimedes."

CHAPTER 20

Atticus looked at them. *"Arch* is Archimedes," he repeated.

Dan stared, his mouth half open. "You mean the Greek dude?" he said.

"What was he, like, a mathematician?" Jake asked.

"Yes, and a scientist and an inventor. One of the greatest who ever lived."

"I get that *Arch* could be short for *Archimedes*," Dan said, "but why are you so sure it's him?"

"A couple of reasons," Atticus said. "First, *antik*. It doesn't mean 'antique.' It's short for *Antikythera*."

"Auntie who?" Dan asked. "This is about Archimedes' aunt?"

"No," Atticus said patiently. "The Antikythera has been called the world's first computer. It was brought up from a shipwreck over a hundred years ago, and people have made replicas of it. It's an amazing device that has all these incredibly complex gears. They think it's an astronomical calendar and that maybe it was invented by Archimedes."

"I'm with you so far," Jake said. "What else?"

"Mali," Atticus said. "The salt artifact—the one with the writing on it?"

"The 'Apology for a Great Transgression,'" Amy murmured.

"Right," Atticus said. "Written by a centurion, a soldier, who felt terrible about killing someone—a really great man. A man whose inventions could have changed the course of history if he'd lived.

"It's been bugging me, because I felt like I'd heard that story. And then just now, when you said the letters were A-R-C-H, something clicked. That's how Archimedes died. He was killed by a soldier."

"Arch . . . Antik . . ." Dan muttered.

He leaned over the folio for another close look just as Amy did the same. They cracked heads.

"OW!" Amy clapped a hand to her forehead. Dan's skull had crashed into hers in exactly the spot that was still tender from head-butting Sinead. Involuntary tears rolled down her cheeks, and she felt momentarily dizzy.

It was one of those bad-timing last straws. Amy flopped onto the bed and turned to one side, her back to the rest of the room.

"You okay?" Jake asked.

She waved him off. "I'll be fine," she managed to say. "I just need . . ." She crossed her arms over her chest, drew her knees up, and huddled into herself.

Without even realizing it, she went to that quiet place in her mind.

How peaceful it was there.

An awkward silence filled the room. All three boys stared at Amy's hunched back for a moment.

Dan cleared his throat. "Um, Amy?"

No response.

Dan leaned over and poked Amy in the back.

Her shoulder twitched once, a tiny gesture, but otherwise she was still.

Worry percolated inside Dan, like bubbles slowly rising to the surface of a thick, noisome sludge he could almost smell.

He tried again. "Come on, you can sleep later. Places to go, people to see!"

Now there was no response at all, even though Dan could see that she wasn't asleep — she was blinking slowly, staring at something he couldn't see.

Don't do this, Amy. Not now. There's too much to do, and we need you.

I *need you.*

Dan could feel his concern for Amy practically radiating out of every pore, which forced him to admit what had been terrifying him since his recovery from the blowpipe attack.

She might crack up. Like, long-term. Or even . . . permanently.

Dan pulled half the bedspread over his sister. The three boys left through the connecting door into the

Rosenblooms' room, with both Jake and Dan giving Amy a last concerned glance over their shoulders.

Jake broke the silence. "What's the plan?" he asked.

Dan stood still a moment longer. He knew it was just his imagination, but he felt as if something had just landed on his shoulders and upper back.

It was a shapeless, nameless mass, but at the same time, so heavy he almost staggered.

If Amy's in no shape to make decisions, someone else has to do it.

Dan tried to swallow, but there was hardly any spit in his mouth.

I guess the job's mine.

Dan's first move was to contact Vesper One with a message that the folio was in their possession. He received an immediate response, which said to get to New York and await further instructions.

Dan sent another text, asking for contact with the hostages. No reply.

He scowled. "I should have asked that first," he muttered.

Jake shook his head. "The answer would have been no anyway," he said.

"I have an idea," Atticus said. "What if you and Amy go to New York to make the drop, and me and Jake try to find out more about the Archimedes connection?"

Dan hesitated. On the one hand, they needed to find out what the Vespers were up to. On the other . . .

"No," he said. "I need to get you back to Attleboro, where you'll be safe from the Vespers. Or at least, safer."

"Listen," Atticus said, his voice pleading. "Two people have gotten hurt because of me — first you and now Dr. Siffright. You can't cut me out of this — can't you see, I have to DO something? And besides, I'm the only one who knows anything about Archimedes."

Doubt prickled Dan's thoughts.

It's funny — I never want Amy to boss me around. But now that she's not, I'm not sure what to do. And it's only been, like, five minutes. How has she done it for so long?

"If you *were* going to research Archimedes, where would you go?" Dan asked.

"Italy," Atticus replied without hesitation. "Sicily, to be specific. That's where he worked."

"I thought he was Greek," Jake said.

"He was. Sicily was part of the Greek empire back then."

Italy, Dan thought. *That's not too far from London. Jonah and Hamilton could be there in, like, a few hours.*

Ham and Jonah researching Archimedes? Not exactly the ideal scenario. Sheesh, how did Amy make up her mind about stuff like this?

"It's not like we have much choice," Dan said aloud. "And if they try and don't come up with anything, we won't be any worse off, right?"

"Who are you talking about?" Jake said.

"Hamilton and Jonah," Dan said. He tapped in the number on his phone.

"Let me talk to them when you're done," Atticus said. "I can give them a few ideas about where to start."

Jonah and Hamilton, having rested up as instructed, were ready to go. Dan told them to send regular updates whether they had any news or not.

Next Dan called the hospital. No change in Dr. Siffright's condition, which Dan chose to see as a good thing. Then he decided to contact their Madrigal connections in Brazil to ask them to keep an eye on her. He was pleased when he thought of this.

Dan went back to the other room. To his immense relief, Amy was up and about, packing her things. He looked at her closely and saw that his relief had been premature: She still had that exhausted, empty look in her eyes and seemed to be moving like a sleepwalker.

"Need any help?" he asked.

"Nope," she said.

"Jonah and Ham are going to Sicily."

"Mmm."

She was "responsive" — wasn't that what TV-show doctors said? And wasn't it always a good thing, as opposed to when a patient was "unresponsive"?

She'll be okay, Dan told himself.

Please, let her be okay.

They retraced their path: a small plane back to São Paulo, then a jet to New York. On the jet, Jake put Atticus in a middle seat, between himself and Dan. Amy sat in the row behind them.

Jake was taking no chances. Maybe Isabel's three attacks were just meant to frighten them. But if the third attack was supposed to be fatal, she had failed — and would surely try again.

"When you go to the bathroom, I go with you," Jake growled at his brother.

He was true to his word. He went into the tiny cubicle and checked it out first; only then did he let Atticus enter. Alone, for which Atticus expressed sarcastic gratitude.

Then Jake waited and walked with Atticus back to their seats, his eyes roving over the other passengers. It was strange how everyone over the age of about twelve looked either suspicious or suspiciously innocent.

Atticus dozed off. Determined not to fall asleep himself, Jake asked Dan for anything he had on the Vespers.

Dan e-mailed him a file. "Take a look at this," he said in a low voice. "That's the list Erasmus got from Mr. McIntyre. I've looked at it a few times, but I can't figure it out."

It was a list of locations. Nothing more, no text or explanation.

Kathmandu	*Tonga*
Sierra de Córdoba	*Manila*
Pompeii	*Kodiak*
Delhi	*Istanbul*
Oakland	*Quito*
Araucania	*Nyanyanu*

There were two places Jake had never heard of—Araucania and Nyanyanu—but he knew the rest.

There's got to be a reason that these are all listed together. Okay, start with the obvious. Pompeii—first thing I think of is the volcano eruption.

Jake's eyes widened.

No way.

It can't be that easy.

He took a breath to calm down and then began mentally ticking off some of the other places on the list.

Delhi, earthquake.

Oakland, earthquake.

Istanbul, earthquake.

Quito, earthquake.

"Subduction zones," he whispered.

He reached across a sleeping Atticus to nudge Dan. "This list," he said, "it's subduction zones. Places where the earth's crust is unstable, where there are fault lines. You know, lots of earthquakes, volcanic eruptions, things like that." Jake stared at the list again. "I don't know them all, but the ones I do know, it's too many to be just a coincidence."

Dan looked over the back of his seat at Amy, who was staring out the window. "Can I see your phone?" he asked politely. They'd all been using a similar tone of voice when talking to her, as if she were made of glass and would shatter if they spoke too loud.

She didn't speak, but gave him the phone. Dan tapped at it. "This is from Ian," he said, showing Jake an e-mail. "He sent it to me after we talked to him at Yale. He was tracking Isabel, remember? And he made a list of places she's been to recently. Supposedly with her charity—Aid Works Wonders. But look at the two lists."

Alaska

Quito

Delhi

Nepal

Istanbul

Jake glanced back and forth between the phone screen and the document on his laptop.

"Quito, Delhi, Istanbul on both lists," Dan said, "but what about the other two?"

"They match, too," Jake said. "Alaska—Kodiak. Nepal—Kathmandu."

"Nice," Dan said. "But what does it mean? Ian says he's sure that the charity is a cover for something else."

"Well, if we assume that Isabel is trying to get to all the places on the Vespers' list—"

Jake saw Dan's face go pale. "Isabel and the Vespers," he whispered. "Isabel must be one."

Jake said, "Sorry, did I miss something? Didn't we

know that already, from the way she's been going after Atticus?"

Dan shook his head. "You don't understand. I don't just mean that she's a Vesper. I mean she must be *One*—Vesper One."

Then a strange expression of what looked like relief seemed to cross Dan's face. "And if she's Vesper One, that means Dad isn't—" He stopped abruptly.

Jake blinked in confusion. "Dad? Whose dad?"

"Never mind," Dan said hastily. "I meant—um, it's bad. Really bad."

Jake shivered.

Isabel in command of the entire Vesper juggernaut was a horror beyond imagining.

Until now, Vesper One had been a frightening, mysterious shadow. But that had changed. V-1 was a known quantity: The Cahills had had far too much experience with the extent of Isabel's ruthlessness. They would need every tool at their disposal to fight her.

And that included the serum.

At least having it on hand, Dan thought for the hundredth time. *Not necessarily using it. But having it, just in case . . .*

One thing Dan knew for sure. They had already lost Phoenix and Alistair. No one else was going to die on his watch. No matter what it took.

So far, Dan had managed to procure thirty-two

Clues; the thirty-third was the serum formula in his head. That meant six were missing. He had to get those and then actually create the serum. To do that, he would need a lab.

The strategy of using Madrigal connections to watch over Dr. Siffright had given him a really good idea. Dan sent several e-mails, and the Madrigal machine kicked into action. By the time the plane landed at Kennedy Airport, Dan had replies assuring him that the remaining ingredients, a lab at Columbia University, and a postdoctoral student in the chemistry department would be at his disposal whenever he needed them.

It was midafternoon in New York, but everyone was exhausted. "We might as well get some sleep until we hear from her again," Dan said.

No one had to ask who he meant.

Jake and Atticus took the room next to Amy and Dan's. Dan lay down on the bed and closed his eyes. But he made himself stay awake until he heard Amy's breathing grow slow and even in sleep. Then he got up and wrote a note:

Amy—couldn't sleep, hanging out with Atticus. —D.

Dan tiptoed out of the room. He knocked quietly on the next door. "It's me," he called softly.

Jake opened the door.

"Amy's asleep," Dan said. "I think we should leave her alone for a while—she really needs to rest."

"No argument from me," Jake said.

"Okay—I'm going to get some sleep, too," Dan said.

He went back to the other room. He set Amy's phone to VIBRATE, then grabbed his backpack. On the way out of the hotel, he stopped at the front desk and asked them to hold all calls.

He hated the thought of leaving Amy alone in the room. But Jake was nearby, and Dan knew he might not have another chance to get away. He'd done what he could to make sure no one would miss him for at least a few hours.

At curbside, Dan sent a text message. Then he hailed a cab.

"Columbia University," he said.

CHAPTER 21

"You sure about this?"

Jonah stared at his reflection in a bathroom mirror at Gatwick Airport, outside London. Hamilton had picked out some new clothes for him: a plain gray T-shirt, dull khaki trousers, and a blue nylon zip-up windbreaker.

"I'm sure," Ham said firmly. "No bling allowed."

"Oh, man," Jonah groaned. "Can't I at least wear something black?"

He was thinking of Erasmus. Erasmus always wore black.

He was trying *not* to think of Phoenix, but his cousin's face hovered at the edge of every thought.

Hamilton sighed. "We've been over this. We've got work to do, and we can't have you drawing crowds everywhere we go. Think of it as — as going undercover."

Undercover. That sounded like something Erasmus would do.

As a worldwide hip-hop star, Jonah had long thought of himself as a pretty cool dude. Now he knew the truth.

Erasmus was beyond cool. Way beyond.

Erasmus wasn't about wearing bling, or how many fans he had, or how much money. That stuff was all outside stuff. Erasmus's kind of cool came from inside.

Jonah hadn't quite figured it out yet, but he was sensing that it had something to do with not caring quite so much about what other people thought.

It was whack: Not caring about being cool was what had made Erasmus so cool.

"Okay," Jonah said. He put on the final item of the disguise, a blue denim baseball cap devoid of logos.

Ham shook his head. "Other way, dude."

Jonah did his best to suppress a scowl of disgust—at both his reflection and Ham—as he turned the cap around so the bill was at the front.

After the flight from London to Palermo, the boys hired a car to take them to a hotel in Syracuse. They arrived in the evening, too late to begin any investigating. The next morning, checking out the hotel's concierge desk, Hamilton found a brochure for a tour with a company that rented Segway personal scooters.

The boys had exchanged several texts with Atticus on the subject of Archimedes and had also researched on their own. There were two places in the city of Syracuse worth investigating: the downtown area called Ortigia and the archaeological district north of there.

"Look," Ham said, showing Jonah the brochure. "The tour starts at the Piazza Archimede and ends at the Tomb of Archimedes. Can't do better than that. You ever ridden one of those Segway things?"

"Yep," Jonah said. "On tour, a couple of years ago. It was way cool because we had a ramp built and did all this fog and lighting stuff—the audience could only see my head and shoulders, and it looked like I was floating down onto the stage." His face fell. "I remember Phoenix saying how awesome it was. . . ."

Hamilton looked at Jonah for a moment. Then he frowned and said, "You think I'll catch on quick enough to keep up with you?"

Jonah blinked a couple of times and squared his shoulders. Then he slapped Hamilton on the back. "It's easy, man—like, five minutes' practice and you'll be good to go."

On hearing Jonah's praise, Hamilton lit up like the human equivalent of a 180-pound Christmas bulb. Jonah was proud of himself. *That's what Erasmus might have done. Quit stewing and get on with things. And don't forget that it hasn't been all cupcakes for Ham, either.*

In the wake of losing both Erasmus and Phoenix, Hamilton had been a rock for Jonah. Sticking more closely than the most dedicated bodyguard, Ham had taken care of everything from travel and hotel arrangements to making sure they ate healthy meals. He even scheduled regular workouts, alternating swims in the hotel pool with weight sessions.

"Exercise releases endorphins," Ham said every time he rousted Jonah out of bed and into workout gear. "And endorphins make you feel good."

The only trouble with the Holt method of recuperation was that it made you feel worse before you felt better. Jonah's muscles hadn't worked this hard in years. And he knew it would take more than a swim or two to get over the losses. But at the moment, none of the Cahills had much time to mourn.

The Vespers' latest deadline felt like bad breath right in their faces.

Piazza Archimede was a traffic roundabout. Cars and trucks circled the piazza at crazed speeds, and it appeared that in Sicilian vehicles, neither the brakes nor the accelerator would work unless the driver was leaning constantly on the horn.

Take away the cars and it could have been another century in the piazza, with its dignified old buildings around a fountain featuring an impressive sculpture. But the statue had nothing to do with Archimedes.

"It's a nymph who got away from some god who was chasing her by turning into a spring," Hamilton said, reading from a brochure.

"A spring? So she could what, boing away?" Jonah asked. It didn't seem like a great way to escape.

"Not that kind of spring," Hamilton said. "The water

kind. And the actual spring is here in Syracuse, too."

"Well, okay, she escapes, but then she has to be a spring for the rest of her life?" Jonah shrugged. "Some of that Greek-myth stuff is lame."

The Segway-rental shop was just off the piazza. As Jonah had predicted, the scooters were easy to get the hang of and the two boys were soon off on an audio tour of Syracuse.

The tour they had chosen lasted three hours. Afraid of missing out on something important, the boys rolled their way through the entire audio file. They learned quite a bit about the city of Syracuse, but relatively little about Archimedes.

At least the Segways were fun. After the first hour or so, Hamilton almost felt like the Segway was part of his body. You made it go by leaning forward and stopped it by leaning back. If you pushed a button on the handlebars and leaned left or right, the scooter would turn the way you wanted it to. It wouldn't do jumps or wheelies or anything cool like that, but for getting around the narrow streets and alleys of Ortigia, it was way better than walking.

Tourists were not allowed inside the Tomb of Archimedes. This was not as big a disappointment as it could have been. "They're not even sure it's his tomb!" Jonah complained.

Archimedes' tomb was indeed somewhere in Syracuse — the Greek philosopher Cicero had found it back in 75 B.C. and written about it — but no one knew where it was now.

"Too bad we didn't know that before we started," Hamilton said. None of the Internet sites he'd researched had been very forthcoming about the Tomb of Archimedes not really being the tomb of Archimedes.

They decided on one more stop: the archaeological museum. It was a huge, very modern structure laid out along the lines of a giant hexagon. Tooling along on their Segways, Jonah and Hamilton followed the signs to the entrance.

Jonah pulled up in a parking area set aside for scooters. One other Segway was parked there, but most of the vehicles were Vespas, the sleek scooters beloved by city-dwelling Italians.

"Jonah, watch this!" Hamilton called from across the parking lot.

He leaned forward and got his Segway up to its top speed of twelve miles per hour. *Steady . . . steady . . . lean a little . . . NOW!*

Hamilton pushed the turn button and leaned hard to his right. In previous attempts, the result had been a neat three-sixty, the forward momentum used up by the spin so the scooter came to a perfect stop. This time, he waited a little too long to go into the turn.

"HAM!" Jonah yelled and jumped out of the way.

Hamilton was inches away from a crash when he leaped off the Segway and sent it barrelling into the row of Vespas. They toppled over like awkward dominoes.

Both boys picked themselves up off the ground. One knee of Jonah's new pants was torn, but he was otherwise undamaged. Hamilton had impressive cases of pavement burn on his right hand and his left elbow.

"You okay?" they said at the same time.

"My bad," Hamilton said as he retrieved his Segway from the pile. Then they began resurrecting the toppled Vespas, eight of them. The scooters were surprisingly heavy.

As they pulled the last of the Vespas upright, Hamilton—or maybe it was Jonah—let go too soon. The scooter fell sideways, knocked into the Vespa next to it, and one by one, the rest of the scooters tipped over again.

"You're kidding," Hamilton said in disbelief.

Jonah groaned. Together they hauled the offending Vespa upright. Then they moved on down the line.

When they reached the last scooter, Hamilton was taking no chances. "Careful with this one," he said. "We don't want the same thing all over. One, two—"

"LADRO!"

A man was running toward them from the museum, waving his arms wildly and pointing at them.

"LADRO!" he yelled again.

Startled, both boys turned toward their accuser and let go of the Vespa—

Which toppled over, and all eight Vespas went down *again*.

CHAPTER 22

Jet lag and general tension added up to a terrible night's sleep for the Cahills and the Rosenblooms. At six in the morning, a message from Vesper One came through. Dan read it aloud:

"'I just adore jewelry. That lovely ring of yours — I simply must have it. In fact, it's the final piece I need to complete my collection. Put the ring and whatever you got from dear Dr. Siffright into a book bag. And come to think of it, I'm hungry. I'd like a nice juicy bacon cheeseburger. Put that in the bag, too. Central Park, Strawberry Fields forever! But in your case, at 8:35 A.M. for a rendezvous with Goldilocks. And of course, don't try to follow her. You know the consequences.'"

The ring.

The Madrigal ring.

It had been protected by Madrigals for centuries, passed along secretly, guarded and protected and valued over life itself. Neither Dan nor Amy knew *why* it was so important, but the fact that Grace had entrusted it to them was all the explanation they needed.

The ring was embedded in Amy's watch, forming the circle around the dial. The watch had been custom-made by a Madrigal/Ekat jeweler, waterproof, shatterproof, fireproof, every other -proof available.

Why did the Vespers want it? What did Vesper One mean by saying it was the "final piece"?

Palms sweaty and throat dry, Dan went into the bathroom for a drink of water. The phone beeped and another transmission came through.

It was a video file showing an extreme close-up of Nellie's face. She looked terrible, her hair limp and greasy, dark crescents under her eyes.

"Hey, kiddos," she said in a whisper.

The entire history of their relationship in two words: Nellie had called them "kiddos" from the first day she met them. Whatever happened, Amy and Dan would always be her kiddos.

Dan had to clear his throat against a lump formed by equal parts love and dread.

The camera pulled away slowly.

He gasped.

There was a gun pointed at Nellie's left temple. The finger on the trigger twitched.

Then the feed cut off.

At around 7:15, Jake called room service and ordered a bacon cheeseburger. There was a brief scare when he was told it was too early in the morning. A considerable tip to be shared between the manager and the kitchen staff resulted in the production of the burger.

When it came up to the room, the smell of it almost made Dan sick.

And I used to love bacon cheeseburgers, he thought.

"What's with the cheeseburger?" Jake asked. "From what you've said about Isabel, I'd have thought she'd ask for champagne and caviar."

"I guess we'll find out soon enough," Atticus said.

Dan hadn't shown the video to anyone else. *What's the point,* he thought, *we can't do anything about it, and this way nobody else needs to feel as bad as I do right now.*

He glanced over at Amy for the thousandth time. She was sitting in a corner chair, her head down. Since their arrival in New York, she had remained in sleepwalk mode — there, but not quite all there. Dan had tried everything to break through the invisible wall that seemed to be surrounding her. He felt his guts twisting slowly and helplessly whenever he looked at her.

Dan tried calling Hamilton and Jonah yet again. Every time, the connection went straight to voice mail. He was desperate for them to uncover something that might give them an idea of what the Vespers' plan was — something the Cahills could use against them.

8:00 A.M.

His heart thudding, Dan began to prepare for the drop. They had already bought a book bag at the hotel gift shop. Atticus held it open while Dan put in the folio and the cheeseburger, wrapped in a napkin.

Now for the hard part, he thought.

He crossed the room to the corner.

"Amy," he said, "I need your watch."

Amy jerked her head up like a wild animal on alert. She clamped her right hand over the watch, her eyes wide with alarm.

"No," she croaked hoarsely. "Grace trusted me."

Dan clenched his fist in a tiny gesture of triumph. *If she knows that much, she's still with me. . . .*

"We have to," he said gently. "Nellie. And Fiske, and the others."

Amy lowered her head and peeked at the watch under her hand, then shook her head violently.

"I can't," she whispered. "Grace . . ."

Dan looked into her eyes. "Amy," he said, "Grace would have understood." He reached for her wrist.

"NO!"

Amy drew up her knees and backed herself farther into the chair, turning sideways and shielding the watch with her body. For a moment Dan wondered if she was going to bare her teeth at him.

Dan found himself trembling. He took a deep breath. *No more Mr. Nice Guy.*

"Amy," he said, his voice firm and loud enough that out of the corner of his eye he saw both Jake and Atticus stiffen. "I need your watch. I promise I'll get it back for you if I can. But you have to give it to me."

One more breath.

"Give it to me NOW."

He was almost yelling at her, and the pain in her eyes was killing him.

It worked. She went limp and held her left arm out weakly toward him. He knelt in front of her, unstrapped the watch, then circled her bare wrist with one hand and gave it a gentle squeeze.

She lowered her other hand to his shoulder, and for a few moments, they both held on tight.

Dan stood with one hand on the doorknob, the book bag over his other arm. It had been decided that he would make the drop on his own. Jake would stay at the hotel, keeping Atticus out of harm's way.

Dan . . . going to meet the Vespers by himself . . .

From somewhere deep inside Amy, words struggled to the surface and broke through. "I'm going with you."

Part of her was surprised to hear her own voice. It was almost as if she were outside her body, observing herself. *Scared Amy and Safe Amy,* she thought. *Safe Amy doesn't want any part of this. She's just watching Scared Amy, who can't let Dan go alone.*

"It's okay," Dan said at once. "We've done this before — it's only a drop. I'll be back before you know it."

"I wasn't asking," Amy said.

All three boys stared at her. She glanced down at her wrist and remembered, with a shock like a jolt to her heart, that her watch was no longer there.

She walked past Jake and Atticus, past Dan, and out the door.

Strawberry Fields was on the west side of Central Park. It was a memorial to the great musician John Lennon, who was once a member of the Beatles and then a celebrated solo artist. The memorial was a circular mosaic embedded in the pavement, with the word *Imagine*—the title of one of Lennon's most famous songs—in the center. "Imagine" was a song about world peace, and the memorial was both a designated quiet zone in the park and a peace garden.

Amy and Dan stood side by side near the mosaic, nervous and watchful. The park wasn't crowded, but there were still plenty of people walking the paths.

Amy could feel Dan looking at her every few seconds while at the same time trying to hide his anxiety.

He's worried about me, thought Scared Amy.

Don't think about anything. Just get this over with, responded Safe Amy.

"Goldilocks," Dan muttered. "I guess that means it will be somebody blond."

Of course, as soon as he said that, it seemed like most of the people they saw were blond. But blond or not, everyone walked past them without a glance.

They had arrived a few minutes early. Amy knew from past drops that the Vesper pickup was nearly always right on time. But 8:35 came and went with no one approaching them.

8:36.

8:37.

8:38.

If I have to wait one more minute, I'm going to go crazy, Amy thought. *Or maybe I already am. . . .* Automatically she began picking at the blister on her neck again.

Just then, a big dog came up to Dan and sniffed him politely.

"Hey there," Dan said and dropped to one knee to pet the dog.

It was a beautiful golden retriever, with a perfectly shaped head and a thick coat of the fur "feathers" characteristic of the breed. Amy bent over to pet the dog, too. Its fur was so soft, its warmth so comforting, she wanted to bury her face in its neck for a good cry.

The dog accepted their greetings, then whimpered gently.

"What is it, girl?" Dan asked quietly.

Amy looked around. "Where's her owner?" she wondered.

The dog nosed the book bag hanging from Dan's arm.

"She smells the cheeseburger," he said. "Sorry, girl, wish we could give you a bite, but the Vespers—"

Amy made a strangled sound as her breath snagged in her throat. They looked at each other and then at the dog.

Dan fumbled for the bone-shaped metal tag that

dangled from the dog's collar. He flipped it over and his jaw dropped. "'Goldilocks.'"

Incredulous, he held out the bag. The dog nosed it again, but was definitely not pawing or ripping into it in search of the cheeseburger.

"She's been really well trained," Dan said, his voice edged with anger.

Goldilocks was now trying to put her head through the handles of the bag.

A wave of bitterness washed over Amy. *It's sick. Using this beautiful, intelligent dog for such evil ends . . .*

She put both handles over the dog's head and adjusted the bag so it hung in front. Goldilocks gave a single bark and then trotted out of the park.

A sob tore its way out of Amy's throat.

Grace, I'm sorry, I'm so so, sorry. . . .

Unable to stop herself, she stumbled a few steps in the direction taken by Goldilocks. But Dan was right beside her, his arm around her shoulders, holding her back and holding her up at the same time.

Amy felt like she might have stayed frozen there forever if her phone hadn't rung.

It was Jonah—finally.

"WHERE HAVE YOU BEEN?" Amy almost screamed into the phone.

Dan snatched the phone away from her. "Amy," he said, *"chill."*

He spoke into the phone. "Jonah, are you somewhere where you can Skype? Okay, we're gonna go back to our hotel now. We'll Skype you in, like, ten minutes. Right. Good."

He gave the phone back to Amy.

Amy said nothing. Together they walked out of the park, with Amy casting a few desperate glances toward where Goldilocks had disappeared.

Dan gave Jake and Atticus a quick summary of the drop. Then he logged in to Skype, holding his breath as he made the connection.

Please let them have found something. For Amy's sake. Something that will tell us what the Vespers are up to — or at least a clue to where the hostages are. Please please please . . .

Jonah and Hamilton appeared on the screen sitting next to each other. "Hi, guys," Dan said, making a supreme effort to stay calm. "What happened? We kept calling you but your phones—"

"Yeah, I know," Jonah said. "Our phones were—well, I guess you could say they were out of commission—"

"What he means," Hamilton said, "is we were *in jail.*"

"What!?"

"Why?"

"What happened?"

"Whoa," Jonah said, holding up his hands. "We've got some important stuff to tell you, so we'll just give you the short version for now. We weren't exactly in jail, but we were at a police station, and they took away our phones."

"This guy thought we were stealing his scooter," Hamilton said. "We weren't, but he kinda went crazy and was yelling, and neither of us speaks Italian—"

"—or Sicilian," Jonah added. "Did you know they speak Sicilian here and it's, like, a whole different thang from regular Italian?"

"It took us ages to explain everything and get it all sorted out, but anyway it turns out this guy—"

"—the same guy, the one with the scooter, and we

forgot to say, it happened at the archaeological museum—"

"He's an Archimedes expert!" Hamilton finished triumphantly.

"Wow," Dan said. "I guess it turned out to be a good thing, you guys stealing his scooter."

"We weren't stealing it!" Jonah said in exasperation. "Anyway, that 'Apology' thing—the document you found in Mali? It fits right in. It turns out that the Romans were invading Syracuse, and the head dude, this guy named Marcellus, had given orders to find Archimedes and bring him in."

"Because Marcellus knew that Archimedes was, like, this major mega-genius," Hamilton said.

Jonah continued, "But what went down was, Archimedes was working on some big project at the time—he was building something, and he had parts and plans scattered all over the place, and when the soldier invaded his house, he was like, no way, I can't come with you right now, I gotta finish what I'm doing here.

"And the soldier kept giving the order and Archimedes kept denyin' him, and finally the soldier got pissed off and killed him!"

"When Marcellus heard that, he was really mad," Hamilton said. "But some people think the soldier didn't know who Archimedes was when he went to arrest him. Anyway, the soldier realized he'd messed up big-time, so that must be why he wrote the 'Apology' thing."

"Right. And for, like, his whole life, Nico's been trying to figure out what Archimedes was working on that day—"

"Wait," Atticus said, "who's Nico?"

"Oh, sorry—that's the scooter guy. We explained everything to him and the police, and then he calmed down, and it turned out his English is pretty good. So we got to talking, and that's how we found out he knows all about Archimedes, and we ended up going to a café with him."

"What else did he tell you?" Jake asked.

"Okay, so Archimedes was working on some device when he got killed, right? But his drawings and the device itself up and disappeared. It was an invasion, and everything was all crazy, but Nico thinks that because everybody knew what a genius Archimedes was, whoever took the stuff wouldn't have trashed it, they'd have kept it safe somehow. Nico thinks that Archimedes was working on something really important. He's spent years looking for any trace of it, and he thinks there might be something in the Archimedes Palimpsest."

"The Palimpsest?" Atticus said. "But they already know what's in that. It's mostly mathematical formulas, about spheres and—"

"Hold up," Dan said. "What's the Palimpsest?"

"Atticus, you explain it to them," Jonah said. "And do you guys have another laptop there? The Palimpsest is online, you should get it up on another screen."

It turned out that the Archimedes Palimpsest was every bit as amazing as the Voynich Manuscript.

"Palimpsests," Atticus said. "I studied them with Mom." He paused for a moment, and Dan was struck by how the brief silence instantly filled with Atticus's yearning for his mom.

He knew what that felt like.

Jake reached out and touched his brother's dread-locks, then turned the caress into a gentle tug.

"Ow," Atticus said absently, but now he was back with them. "Okay, in ancient times, manuscripts were written on vellum, which was made from animal hides, right? Vellum was expensive, so they found ways to reuse it. What they would do is, take an old manuscript and scrape off all the ink, and then they'd write new stuff on it.

"A palimpsest is an *original* manuscript—the one that got scraped off. Of course, in those days, nobody could read a palimpsest. I mean, that was the whole idea, to get rid of the old writing so you could reuse the vellum."

"You mean, nowadays you *can* read them? How?" Dan asked. He almost added, *Does it say where the hostages are?* but he stopped himself. Stupid questions would just waste precious time. Time—how long had it been since the drop? Why hadn't the Vespers made contact? *"The final piece"*—maybe the hostages were being released at that very moment. . . .

Yeah, right, Dan thought bitterly.

"Technology," Atticus answered his question. "If there was iron in the original ink, they can pick up traces of it by using X-rays. Plus there are color-enhancement techniques and all kinds of stuff they can try now. It's not, like, crystal clear or anything. But they can read some of it and guess at the rest."

"I've got it here," Jake said. He put Atticus's laptop next to Dan's.

At digitalpalimpsest.org, there were hundreds of fascinating images. Atticus explained that the Archimedes Palimpsest was essentially a thirteenth-century Byzantine prayer book. Underneath it, scholars had found much older manuscripts, including several of Archimedes' works.

"They're from the tenth century," Atticus said. "Archimedes died in 212 B.C. None of the works he wrote—I mean, that he actually *wrote*, with his own hand—have survived. The Palimpsest is the oldest known copy."

"They're a mess!" Dan exclaimed, looking at the images over Jake's shoulder. "It's hard to make out anything at all!"

The digital images showed the layers of ink. The top layer of writing was clear and strong, even after more than six hundred years. The oldest, bottom layer was extremely faint, sometimes barely discernible despite all the enhancements.

"Yeah, that's why it's taking Nico so long to do his

research," Jonah said from the other screen. "He's examining those images, like, a quarter inch at a time."

"The thing about Archimedes' devices is, they were *way* ahead of his time," Hamilton said. "There's this thing called the Archimedes screw, for getting water out of the hold of a big boat, right? He invented it more than two thousand years ago and they're STILL using it today!"

"Yeah, Nico kept saying that over and over," Jonah said, "how incredible Archimedes was, almost like he could see into the future. There's this device called the Antikythera—"

"Atticus told us about that," Dan cut in. He was finding it all but impossible to control his impatience for some good hard info. "Is that what he was building?"

"No. I mean, Nico isn't for sure about that. But there are a bunch of diagrams of circles, he thinks are gears. They're really cool—they form these perfect triangles—"

"Gears?"

Amy spoke for the first time in the whole conversation.

"Jonah, did you say *gears*?" she asked.

CHAPTER 24

Amy had been listening to every word. She knew that this conversation was an important one. But she was fighting hard against the desire to sink into the comfort of that safe place. The word *gears* was like a hand trying to haul her out of a bog.

The image on the folio . . .

"Yeah, dozens of them," Jonah was saying. "Way more accurate and precise than anything else from the same period. But they've made reproductions of the Antikythera, and it's so complete and, like, perfect, Nico is pretty sure it wasn't what Archimedes was working on when he got offed."

"So we still don't know why the Vespers wanted the folio," Dan said.

"We're not done yet," Hamilton said. "Just listen."

"Well, because some of those circle drawings look a lot like the Antikythera gears," Jonah said, "Nico thinks Archimedes was using them as a basis for another device. Go check out the section about war machines."

"Huh?" Atticus was clearly flummoxed. "What are you talking about—there's nothing about war machines in the Palimpsest."

"It's new," Hamilton said. "I mean, not new—it's as old as the other ones, but they only uncovered it a little while ago."

"Yeah, with the technology, they've found more documents than they thought were there at first," Jonah said.

Jake found the section titled "On Inventions for Battle." He clicked through the images, zooming in occasionally whenever he saw a circular drawing.

Amy got up from her chair and went to look over his shoulder. She could smell him—a healthy boy smell. For some reason, it brought tears to her eyes that she had to blink away.

"Archimedes invented a bunch of cool weapons," Jonah was saying. "Really fly catapults to fling stones at the invaders, and also giant cranes with grappling hooks to pick up ships in the harbor."

"It was awesome," Hamilton said. "So there's Syracuse, this little city, being attacked by the superpowerful Roman army, right? And Archimedes' weapons were so good that the Romans had to take it by siege instead, and it took almost three years!"

Suddenly, Dan sat up straighter and said, "Wait—look!" He pointed to the screen and yelled, "BINGO!"

The page contained both text and drawings. The drawings were of gears.

"Those look just like—" Jake started to say.

"They *are* just like!" Dan said, who was now standing up. "They're *exactly the same* as the ones on Folio Seventy-four. But what does it mean?" He jiggled from one foot to the other, excitement and impatience and frustration flying off him like sparks.

Then Amy inhaled quickly.

"Zoom in there," she said, her voice low and tense. Her hand shaking, she pointed to a drawing near the left margin that looked like little more than a doodle.

The line on the Voynich folio—the one that led to a five-pointed star. The star appeared to indicate the location of something important.

But what?

Now Amy was staring at the doodle. Like everything Archimedean in the Palimpsest, it was faded, faint, chicken-scratchy, buried under the top layer of writing. About half an inch long, it was sort of a curved bar marked by notches. The details were almost impossible to make out—unless you knew what it was.

Amy knew. She'd have known it anywhere. She had seen it dozens, maybe hundreds of times a day, every day for years now.

It was a sketch of a small part of the Madrigal ring.

They were so close. Dan could feel it. *Not just in my gut, but in my liver and my spleen and my—my pancreas, too. If I knew where that was.*

We HAVE to figure out what Archimedes wrote on that page!

Despite frantic searches on all available laptops and phones, the group could not locate any transcriptions of the Palimpsest text online.

"Why can't we find it?" Dan yelled. He was tearing at his hair, something he had read about but never actually done before.

"It's probably because there are some books that have the transcriptions," Atticus said, "and they must be copyrighted or something."

"Atticus, you know Latin," Jake said urgently. "Can you read what's on that page?"

"Oh, man," Atticus said. "I doubt it. It's so hard to make out—it's gonna take me a while."

Dan made a quick decision. "We'll go to the coffee shop to give you some peace and quiet," he said.

"Not me," Jake said. "I'll be standing right outside the door, baby bro."

Atticus worked his way through the dense Latin text on the page with the sketch of the ring. Many letters were illegible, and even those he could read were difficult to string together into words.

Have to find it, whatever it is. It's up to me. . . . Dan and Dr. Siffright were hurt because of me. . . .

After half an hour, the muscles in his neck and shoulders felt like they had been macraméd by tension and strain. He sagged in the chair. *This is taking way too long — we don't have this kind of time. I need to get through it faster somehow. Brainstorm ideas, that's what Mom would say if she were here.*

Atticus's insides contracted a little at the thought of his mom. At the same time, he was comforted by the thought of her cheering him on.

Atticus took the hotel pen and pad from the desk drawer and made some notes.

— *astrolabe*

— *'Apology'*

— Book of Ingenious Devices

— *Voynich folio*

— *Madrigal ring*

These were the things Vesper One had ordered them to turn over. Atticus then did some quick research online about each item.

Vespers 101B, the refresher course, he thought to himself grimly. He also investigated a few sites about Archimedes and related topics.

After this brief respite from the grainy images of the Palimpsest itself, Atticus was ready to go back to it. Only a few minutes in, he was having much more success than he had earlier.

Then he came to some words that took his breath away as effectively as a gut punch.

Machina . . . fini . . . mundi . . .

"No," he croaked aloud. "Oh, no . . ."

CHAPTER 25

In the coffee shop, Amy was sitting facing the door, so she was the first to see Atticus shuffle in almost as if it was hurting him to walk. His face was wan and his eyes dark with shock. Amy's stomach rippled with sudden nausea.

Jake was right behind him. As they neared the table, he stopped a passing waitress.

"Coffee," he said, "very milky and lots of sugar, please."

Amy had never seen Atticus drink coffee, but maybe Jake thought his brother needed it now.

Atticus sat down and said nothing for a few moments. Amy looked at Jake and saw a combination of impatience and dread on his face, exactly what she herself was feeling. Atticus had apparently not told him anything yet.

The coffee arrived and Atticus downed half of it in a few scalding gulps. Then, still gripping the cup tightly, he began speaking, his voice raspy with tightness.

"The stuff they made us steal," he said, "most of

it has to do with Archimedes. And his devices. And besides those things, other stuff has gone missing. Some super-powerful magnets. And the Antikythera itself—a replica was stolen from a museum a few months ago."

He paused and peered into the coffee cup as if hoping to find one of the missing objects there.

"I figured out some of the words on the page with the ring—*magnet*, and *Earth's crust* and *disaster*. Archimedes was theorizing that if you focused on subduction zones—places where the earth's crust is unstable—and used a device equipped with really powerful magnets, you could create disasters like earthquakes and volcano eruptions."

He turned the cup nervously in his hands. "He writes that he's planning to make the device based partly on the workings of the Antikythera. And then it says '*machina fini mundi.*'"

Atticus blinked a few times and swallowed hard. "It means 'machine for the end of the world.' Otherwise known as a doomsday device."

He looked up at Jake, his expression almost pleading—as if maybe his big brother could make it all go away.

"The Vespers have been stealing plans and parts to make Archimedes' doomsday device."

Amy pressed her hands to her temples, hard, but she couldn't stop the visions of massive disasters parading through her mind. Earthquakes, tsunamis, collapsing skyscrapers and highway bridges, raging fires. Hordes of people running and screaming, bloodied from injuries, blank-eyed in shock and desperation. Dead bodies tangled in mass graves, or clogging rivers, or laid out in endless lines under shrouds . . .

That's what I've done. That's what I've given them the ability to do.

Amy felt the burning acid of bile rise in her throat.

"The 'final piece,'" she said, choking out the words. "Grace's ring. The last thing they needed to finish the doomsday device. And I just gave it to them."

She had traded the lives of thousands, maybe *millions* of innocent strangers, for five of her family and friends.

Five.

If she had known about the doomsday device, would she have given up the ring? Or would she have hung on to it, hidden it, maybe even destroyed it, to save the rest of the world—losing Nellie and Fiske and the others forever?

The blister on her neck seemed to be pulsing; she'd been picking at it again. She gave it yet another scratch.

It burst.

A tiny painful explosion of blood and pus left a loose flap of skin, with the tender flesh underneath exposed and raw.

Oblivious to the wound that was seeping drops of blood onto her collar, Amy rose from her chair and walked toward the door of the coffee shop—not the

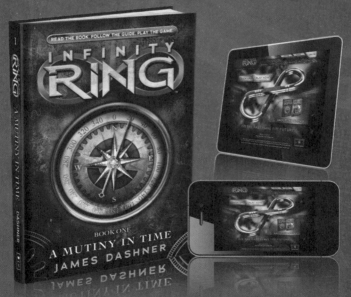

Hello Cahill Friends!

Your services are no
longer required.
Have a nice life!
On second thought, that
won't be happening.
What should I say instead?

Have a nice death!

Vesper One